A
Different Twist

Other Apple Paperbacks
you will enjoy:

A
Different Twist

by Elizabeth Levy

Based on a teleplay by
Dianne Dixon

AN
APPLE
PAPERBACK

SCHOLASTIC INC.
New York Toronto London Auckland Sydney

ISBN 0-590-44317-8

12 11 10 9 8 7 6 5 4 3 2   4   3 4 5 6/9

Printed in the U.S.A.   28

Contents

A
Different Twist

Chapter 1

The Chance of a Lifetime

Christi knew her voice was unusual. She had a big, powerful voice and almost perfect pitch. Her voice made her sound more grown up than she looked—and felt! She was almost twelve, but she wasn't boy crazy the way some of her friends were getting, going on about "hunks." Luckily her best friend, Lizbeth, wasn't into boys yet either. In fact, they both agreed that all boys were turkeys, except for Phil Grey. He definitely wasn't a turkey. Phil Grey was different. First of all, he wasn't really a boy. He was a man and simply the best singer-dancer in the world. Both Christi and Lizbeth had posters of him on their walls, but they had made a pledge to each other not to call him a hunk. Christi fantasized that someday *she'd* make it in show business, and then Phil Grey would really notice her.

But right now, she had to be satisfied with a solo part in the glee club. She stood in the front line licking her lips. She listened to the singers behind her. They sounded good, but they were a fraction behind the beat. She'd have to decide whether to sing her solo off speed or to pick it up.

She glanced at Ms. Cartwright, the glee club director and one of her favorite teachers. Ms. Cartwright was throwing herself into the song, "Imagine," by John Lennon.

Ms. Cartwright was a Beatles fanatic. She was convinced that centuries from now Lennon and McCartney's songs would still be sung, their music would survive the way Mozart's music still gave pleasure. "Sing it as if you're singing for an audience in the year 2490," she had said.

"Yeah, sing it for the mutants, they're the only ones who will be alive then," muttered Lizbeth.

Christi told her to hush. She liked the image of singing for the future. It made the music fresh. Even though this was just rehearsal, Christi liked to try to vary her interpretation, to try it a new way. She liked Ms. Cartwright just because she challenged them all the time.

Christi belted out her solo, putting herself into it, like John Lennon had said, "Imagine . . . a world without hate or fear . . ." For several seconds, Christi forgot about everyone else in the room.

Then it was over and Christi came back down to earth. She was back at school, back in room 254, a soundproof practice room filled with more girls than boys because too many boys thought glee club was sissy. The boys made Christi mad because the glee club would have sounded better with more male voices in it.

She glanced over at Tony DiSpirito, one of the few boys who did sing. Tony was certainly not stupid, not by a long shot. She didn't know him well; he was in the other fifth grade class, but she knew that Tony had the best male voice in the glee club, and he had wanted her solo.

Ms. Cartwright put down her baton. "That was wonderful! Christi, you did a great job with your solo."

Lizbeth winked at Christi. "I bet they heard you in the year 2490," she whispered.

Christi grinned. "Yeah, I'm a time space machine."

"Make that a space cadet," said Tony.

"Takes one to know one," snapped Christi, wishing she could have thought of something wittier to say.

Tony laughed.

Christi felt herself blush. How could she have

said something so stupid? She should have just ignored Tony. He was the turkey of the turkeys.

"Don't mind him," whispered Lizbeth. "You were great!"

Ms. Cartwright tapped her baton on the lectern. "Before the bell rings, I have an exciting announcement to make. There are going to be auditions for a special production of *Oliver!* at the Civic Center."

Tony stopped chattering. He gave Ms. Cartwright his widest smile. "They're wasting their time. They don't need to audition anyone else. I'm available. Tell them Tony DiSpirito accepts the part of Oliver."

Ms. Cartwright smiled. "What? . . . And give up your career as class clown? Even Phil Grey wouldn't demand that kind of sacrifice. That's why he's cast the show with professional actors."

There was complete silence in the room.

Lizbeth raised her hand. "Did you say Phil Grey?" she whispered. "Phil Grey?" Lizbeth glanced at Christi.

Ms. Cartwright nodded her head. "You heard me right. Phil Grey. He's decided he wants to try his hand at directing in a nonthreatening atmosphere. I guess he thinks our town is nonthreatening. Anyhow, he's bringing in his own people for the leads, but he wants local kids for the urchin chorus. I know how some of you feel about

4

Phil Grey . . . in fact, I feel that way, too. I wish there was some way that I could disguise myself as a kid. I'd try out too."

Nearly every night before Christi went to sleep, she fantasized about meeting Phil Grey. She had a whole card catalogue of daydreams about how she and Phil Grey met. Usually they involved Christi tripping over him in an airport. She had never even dared to fantasize that he would show up in her own town.

Christi knew that she would get into that urchin chorus. She just had to. Phil Grey would decide to take her under his wing. He'd want to record a duet with her. He'd make her a star, complimenting her on her unspoiled style. He'd tell her never to change.

Christi was so lost in her new daydream that she hardly noticed that Lizbeth was poking her in the ribs with her elbow. "Phil Grey . . . Phil Grey . . . coming here. It's unreal!"

Christi shook her head. "It's fate," she whispered.

"When are the auditions, Ms. Cartwright?" asked Tony. "I gotta get myself ready." He grinned. "Of course, it's a bit of a come down for me, just to be in the chorus."

Christi stared at him. Tony would be her competition. What if he got in and she didn't?

Ms. Cartwright rummaged around in the music

5

on her desk. "I've made copies of the information sheet. I think you should all try out. It's a chance of a lifetime. The auditions are tomorrow. I'm sure the exact time is on the sheets."

Ms. Cartwright passed out the sheets. Christi took hers. Her hands were shaking. Ms. Cartwright paused in front of her. "Good luck!" she whispered.

Chapter 2
You'll Never Know How Cute He Is

Lizbeth poked Christi when they got to their lockers. "Earth to spaceship . . . are you there?"

Christi came out of her daydream. "Lizbeth, can you believe it? He's coming here . . . here! We have a chance to really work with him. He'll get to know us." Christi opened her locker, the door was covered with her collection of Phil Grey pictures, particularly the one of him in a tuxedo jacket with no shirt on underneath. He was peeling off one white glove and he held a cane under his arm.

Lizbeth stared at the picture thoughtfully. "Do you think he's as cute in person as he is in the movies?"

"Yes," said Christi dreamily.

Unfortunately, Tony and his friend Dennis were at the locker next to Christi. "Too bad you'll never find out," said Tony in a mocking voice.

Lizbeth whirled around. "Tony, mind your own business, okay?"

Tony sidled over to them, deliberately raising his voice. "I don't know how cute Phil Grey is, but he sure is smart."

"Yeah, real smart," echoed Dennis, who usually played second banana to Tony. "He's not letting girls try out for his play."

"Very funny," snapped Christi. She knew she had a better chance of making the chorus than Dennis, maybe even a better chance than Tony. Dennis was probably just scared and couldn't help making dumb jokes.

"It's a tragedy," said Tony. "You'll never know how cu-u-ute he is." Tony mimicked Lizbeth's voice perfectly.

"It's so sad," mocked Dennis, wiping away a fake tear. Both boys leaned against their lockers and put on a great show of phony weeping and wailing mixed with equal parts of barely contained laughter.

Christi slammed her locker shut, not really focusing on the guys or what they were saying. She knew they just loved to tease girls. It was

Tony DiSpirito's favorite occupation.

"Come on, Lizbeth," said Christi. "They're just jealous because they know we'll get into the chorus and they won't. Phil Grey is too smart to hire creeps for his show, especially boy creeps."

"Oh yeah, Miss Smarty," said Tony.

"*Ms*. Smarty to you. . . . Tony, why don't you grow up." Christi grabbed Lizbeth's arm.

Tony stopped them. He pulled out the *Oliver!* information sheet from his pocket. He grinned from ear to ear as he handed it to Christi with an exaggerated flourish. "Check out the very last sentence."

"Yeah," said Dennis, clearly relishing the moment. "Only try not to cry will you, especially on the announcement. We need it."

Reluctantly, Christi took the paper from Tony. She gave Tony a suspicious look. To her surprise, he looked embarrassed and almost a little sorry for her. It was the pity in his eyes that scared her. What if Tony was telling the truth!

Quickly Christi scanned the page. Lizbeth hopped up and down beside her, trying to get a look at the paper. "What does it say? What does it say?" screamed Lizbeth.

Finally Christi focused her eyes. She looked at the last two lines on the announcement. How could Ms. Cartwright have missed it? "I can't believe it," she muttered to herself. "It's true."

She looked up from the paper and crumpled it in her hand. Lizbeth gulped.

"It's true?"

Christi nodded. "It says, 'Boys only in the urchin chorus.' "

Dennis giggled nervously, but Tony shushed him up. He took the crumpled paper from Christi's hand. Christi watched them go down the hall.

"Boys only!" groaned Lizbeth, taking out her own copy of the announcement. "It's not fair. *Boys* don't even think Phil Grey is cute!"

"It's not that he's cute that's so important," added Christi. "It's that he's so good. Think of what we could learn from him."

"I'm thinking!" said Lizbeth. "I'm thinking."

"Not that," giggled Christi. "I meant professionally. He could teach us so much. We'd be professionals like him. It's unfair. It's unequal opportunity!"

"It certainly is!" said Lizbeth. "To think blocks of wood like Dennis or Tony will meet him and we won't. They couldn't care less. And I've already planned the outfit to wear to the audition."

"Your glitter sweater and miniskirt," said Christi.

Lizbeth nodded. "How did you guess?"

Christi laughed. " 'Cause you wear it every chance you get."

Lizbeth looked sad. "Now, Phil Grey will never get to see me in it. *It's not fair!*"

"What's unfair?" asked JoAnne and Melody, two girls from their class.

"Phil Grey is unfair."

"I thought you two were the Phil Grey freaks in our class," said JoAnne. "Personally, I think he's dullsville."

"Dullsville!" exclaimed Lizbeth.

"You wouldn't say that if you were a boy and had a chance to be in his chorus," said Christi.

"Who cares?" said Melody. "I'd rather watch him on the stage. I heard he's doing *Oliver!* at the Civic Center. My parents have already got seats. Come on, we'll be late for class."

Lizbeth stared at them. "Imagine thinking Phil Grey is dullsville."

"JoAnne said that just to get you mad," said Christi. "You always let her and Melody get to you. Forget them. We've got to figure out a way to get into those auditions. Maybe we can sue them for sex discrimination."

Lizbeth looked doubtful. "Somehow I don't think so. What if the play calls for all boys. I think it does."

"It doesn't matter," argued Christi. "They should have girl urchins as well as boy urchins." Christi looked down at the announcement again, as if

11

expecting the print to change before her eyes. "Maybe it is a misprint," she said wistfully.

Lizbeth looked hopeful. "Hey, that's not a bad idea."

"What?" asked Christi. "It didn't sound like much of an idea. It was more like a faint hope."

"I know, but suppose we pretend that we haven't read the fine print. We can sign up for the auditions and pretend we didn't realize it was for boys only."

Christi looked doubtful. "What good will pretending do us? They still won't let us in."

"Maybe we can talk our way in. At the very least, we'll get a chance to meet Phil Grey." Lizbeth grinned. "Once Phil Grey hears your voice, he'll want you in the show. He'd be crazy not to. You've got the best voice around here."

"I'm not so sure about that. Tony DiSpirito's voice is pretty good."

"But Tony can't act as well as you can," argued Lizbeth. "You're a double threat. You can sing and act."

"Yeah, but I'm still a girl," said Christi.

Chapter 3

Out of Luck!

After school Christi and Lizbeth rode their bikes downtown to the Civic Center. They locked them up just as a large van pulled up to the backstage area.

Lizbeth looked around the half empty parking lot.

"What are you looking for?" asked Christi.

"Don't you think he'd have a sports car," said Lizbeth.

"Who?"

"Phil Grey, dummy, who else?"

Christi looked around the parking lot. "I'm just glad it's not full. Maybe not many kids are going to try out and they'll have to take us."

Lizbeth took one last look around. "I'm sure he

drives a Porsche or something like that. I bet he's not even here."

"If he's coming to our town because he hoped nobody would make a fuss, maybe he's driving a Plymouth."

"Don't be silly. He wouldn't be caught dead in a Plymouth."

As if on cue, an old beat-up Chevrolet with a Rent-A-Wreck sticker on its rear window pulled up and parked in an empty space near the backstage entrance.

Phil Grey's long legs came out of the car first. He was wearing Nike running shoes that looked like they had gone too many miles. It only took him seconds to get out of the car, but the seconds seemed like a lifetime to Christi. She grabbed Lizbeth's arm and pointed.

Phil Grey turned around. He saw Christi pointing at him, frowned, and hurried into the building through the stage door.

Christi put her hand to her mouth. "Oh, no! It was him, and he saw me pointing at him. I could die!"

Lizbeth stared at the now closed door. "Was it really him? Are you sure?"

"Of course I'm sure. Couldn't you tell? Who else looks like that? Oh, Lizbeth . . . I'm so embarrassed. I feel like such an idiot."

"You're overreacting, calm down. He must be

used to being pointed at. He's Phil Grey."

"I know, but I should have been cool. I don't want him to think I'm just another dingbat who points at him. I want him to think I'm special."

"He will," said Lizbeth. "Come on, let's go try out for that chorus."

"I thought you were the one who said we didn't have a chance."

"I did, but now that I know he's really here, we'll find a way to get in somehow."

Christi hung back. "What if he recognizes me as the stupid kid who pointed at him?" Then she shook her head. "You're right. I'm being a turkey. What am I going on like this for? We've got to go in there and show him what we can do."

"That's the spirit," said Lizbeth. "Only wait a minute, let me comb my hair first."

Christi tapped her foot impatiently while Lizbeth made sure that every strand of her hair was perfect. She wore her curly hair in pigtails, changing the ribbons every day with her outfit. She wanted to wear corn-rows, but her mother wouldn't let her, telling her that it was bad for her scalp. Lizbeth thought her mother just wanted her to be unfashionable.

Christi ran her hand through her red hair. She knew it was messy, but there was little she could do with it. It was thin and straight. Her last haircut had been a "layered" look. She had started growing out her bangs, but they hung in her face. Christi sighed and patted her hair. It would never look as cute as Lizbeth's, so she might as well not worry about it. She would make it on her voice or nothing.

A woman stood by the backstage door with a clipboard in her hands. Christi tried to slip by her, but the woman stepped in front. "Where do you think you're going?" the woman asked, not unpleasantly, but with a weary tone of voice as if she had been fending off preteen girls all day.

Christi cleared her throat. "We're here for the auditions for the urchin chorus."

The woman shook her head. "Sorry . . . it's for boys only."

"You've got to be kidding! We can't even try out?" exclaimed Christi as if this news was a total shock to her.

The woman shook her head as if slightly amused by Christi's acting ability. "That's right. You can't." She gently turned them towards the door. "The script calls for boys only in the urchin chorus."

Lizbeth started out the door, obviously willing to accept defeat, but Christi dug in her heels. "I can play a boy. I've always had a low voice. Oh please . . ."

The woman laughed. "I'm sure you are a good actress," she said in a slightly patronizing voice.

"But Phil says boys only and that's because the script says, 'boys of the urchin chorus.' Your complaint belongs with the author, not with me.

"But an author's words are meant to be changed," said Christi quickly. "In Shakespeare's time boys played girls all the time. Why not vice-versa? Oh, give me a chance. It'll be women's solidarity."

The woman looked at Christi. "I'm a woman. You're a girl," she said.

"But it's terribly unfair," urged Christi. "You must agree. Maybe if we talked to Phil Grey. Couldn't we just see him? Maybe he'd change his mind."

The woman laughed out loud. "I've got to give you credit, no one else has come up with your line, but you can't see Phil, and you can't try out. Sorry." The woman emphatically pushed them out the door.

Desperately, Lizbeth searched the backstage area for just a glimpse of Phil Grey. "Even if he won't change his mind, couldn't we just *see* him."

The woman took a firmer grip on both their arms. "*No*," she said. "For the last time . . . it's *boys only*! You're out of luck!"

Chapter 4
For Girls Everywhere!

Christi slammed her helmet on her head. She unlocked her bicycle and swung her leg over the crossbar. Her parents had insisted that she get a boys bike because they thought it was more sturdy, and they also insisted she wear a helmet every time she rode. Christi glared at the backstage door as if she wished she had superpowers to burn it down. Then she took off at full speed.

Lizbeth got on her bike and tried to keep up with her. "Hey, hold up," she yelled.

"Sorry," said Christi, slowing down. "I was just so mad that I couldn't help myself."

"That was obvious," said Lizbeth, glad for a chance to catch her breath. They coasted down a hill at a more reasonable pace. "What a drag!"

"It's not fair," said Christi.

"I think we've said that before. It doesn't help."

"You're right. When something's not fair, what do you do?"

"You're not thinking of organizing a protest march, are you?" asked Lizbeth. "I don't think Phil Grey would like that. I think we have to admit defeat. You heard what that lady said. There isn't any way. Just forget it."

"Forget Phil Grey, are you crazy? I'm not going to miss a chance to work with him just because I'm a girl."

"I don't think you've got a choice, Christi. You tried. What more can you do?"

"There's got to be a way," insisted Christi.

"You sound like one of those inspirational movies—the girl's crippled but she still runs the marathon. Forget it. All the wishing in the world isn't going to make you a boy. Besides, think about having to spend two whole weeks with nothing but a bunch of smelly, loudmouth boys . . . that would be too gross."

Christi put her feet down and skidded to a halt. Lizbeth almost crashed into her. "What did you say?"

"I said that being with boys all week would be gross."

"No, before that."

"That boys smell."

"No, before that . . ."

"Christi . . . I don't remember every word I say."

"You said that wishing wouldn't make me a boy."

"Yeah." Lizbeth looked at Christi as if she were going bonkers. "You aren't a boy. I happen to have seen you naked. It's a little fact I picked up in biology. I'm sorry if it comes as a shock to you . . ."

Christi laughed. "Lay off the sarcasm. I know I'm not a boy. I don't want to be one, except to get into this play. But maybe I can do more than wish," said Christi slowly. "You said it yourself. I'm a good actress."

Suddenly Lizbeth stared at Christi. "Christi Bay . . . don't even think about it!"

Christi grinned. "If boys could play girls' parts in Shakespeare's time, why can't I play a boy? And nobody has to know. I'll need the right disguise."

Lizbeth looked depressed. "No. You're nuts. It'll never work."

"I'm desperate. It's got to work. You could try it, too."

"No way. I'm not that desperate."

Christi grabbed Lizbeth's arm. "Would you help me?" she begged. "I'll need help."

"You are going to need it. I'll tell you what.

Come to my house early in the morning before school. We'll get you ready for the audition. But if it works, you've got to figure out a way to introduce me to Phil Grey."

"I will. Oh, Lizbeth, do you think I can get away with it?"

"We've got a lot of work to do. It's not going to be easy."

"Lizbeth, you're wonderful. You're terrific to do this for me."

"It's not just for you. It's for girls everywhere."

Christi looked doubtful. "Somehow, I don't think getting me into a boys' chorus ranks up there as a cause."

"You're wrong. Girls should have a right to get as close to Phil Grey as they want."

Christi laughed. "What a slogan."

"Are you going to tell your folks what you're doing?" asked Lizbeth.

Christi frowned. "I don't know. What do you think I should do?"

"I wouldn't tell them," said Lizbeth. "At least not right away. They might not want you to do it. Why don't you worry about that once you get the part?"

"You mean 'if' I get the part."

"Right, why get them all hot and bothered if it turns out you don't make it?"

"I hate to lie to them. Maybe I can just tell

21

them that I'm trying out for the chorus. That isn't a lie. I don't have to tell them that the tryouts are for boys only."

"That's right," agreed Lizbeth. "I'll see you tomorrow. Be there early."

Christi rode Lizbeth home and then she continued slowly back towards her home. She didn't feel quite right. It was true she wasn't about to lie to her parents, but she wasn't exactly going to tell them the truth either. Then she decided she was being silly. First, she'd have to see if she and Lizbeth could pull off the neatest trick of the year—turn a girl into a boy overnight.

Chapter 5
Don't Be So Nice

Christi's parents owned a flower shop called Aaahh Flowers! Christi's mother had come up with the name because they wanted a name that would be first in the yellow pages.

Both her mom and dad worked at the shop all day, and Christi often helped out in the afternoons, making deliveries on her bike, helping with the arrangements, or waiting on customers. It was hard work. But Christi loved the shop. She loved the moist, fragrant smell that hit you as soon as you opened the door.

Her mother was waiting on Mrs. Baker as Christi came in. Mrs. Baker was a widow, who always bought one flower, usually something inexpensive like a daisy. However, she took as much time picking out that one stem as would a customer buying a ten dollar bouquet.

Mrs. Bay never rushed Mrs. Baker. She knew that she was lonely, and picking out her flower for the week was one of her major decisions. Mrs. Baker held two Gerbera daisies up, one a shocking pink, the other a bright yellow. She looked confused.

"I just don't know," she said. "The yellow goes with my furniture . . . but the pink just calls out to me." She turned around, and noticed Christi. "What do you think, dear?"

"I'd take the pink," said Christi seriously. "It's a beautiful pink . . . and if it calls out to you . . . maybe it means you'll have a week in the pink."

Mrs. Baker laughed. " 'A week in the pink,' I like that. I'm surprised a young girl like you knows that phrase."

"Well, I don't really know what it means," admitted Christi. "But it means something good, doesn't it?"

Mrs. Bay tried hard not to laugh. "Very nice. It means a week of being in the pink of health."

"Well, that would be nice for a change," said Mrs. Baker.

Christi started to wrap the pink flower in tissue paper.

Mrs. Baker hesitated, "Do you think I made the right decision?"

"Absolutely," said Mrs. Bay quickly. Christi nodded.

After Mrs. Baker left, Christi gave her mom a kiss. "Where's Dad?"

"He's in the back, working on an arrangement for the Rotary Club luncheon. How was school today?"

"Okay . . . I sang my solo for the glee club. It went well."

"I knew it would. You've been sounding terrific every time you've practiced it."

Christi picked up a stray fern and was about to put it back in a pot when her father came out, carrying a large yellow-and-white arrangement. "How does that look?" he asked. "Last week they complained it wasn't full enough, even though they don't want to spend any more money. . . . Oh, hi, Christi, I didn't hear you come in."

Christi gave the arrangement a critical look. "It does look a tiny bit skimpy."

Mr. Bay groaned. "If they want full, they should pay for full."

"How about just adding a couple of ferns," said Christi. "I just happen to have one right here." Christi stuck it into the arrangement and quickly put in a few others. Suddenly the arrangement looked much more natural and beautiful.

"Perfect," said Mrs. Bay. "You're turning into quite the helper. You should have seen her flattering Mrs. Baker."

"Better her than me," said Mr. Bay. He was a big man with curly red hair and wire-rimmed glasses. He had a great sense of humor but, every once in a while, the constant dealing with his customers got him down. Christi's parents worked very long hours trying to make a living from the flower shop.

"Christi sang her solo today in glee club," said Mrs. Bay. "It went well."

"Imagine all the people," sang Christi's dad slightly off key.

"Well, we know Christi didn't get her voice from you," said Christi's mom laughing.

Christi helped her father move the large arrangement into the van. "I'm glad your solo went well today," he said. "Glad that somebody in the family has some talent."

"You've got lots of talent, Dad."

"But just not as a singer." He closed the door to the van and walked back into the shop with his arm lightly around Christi's shoulder.

"Come on, tell the truth," teased her father. "Don't you think I have a terrific voice?"

"Absolutely," said Christi.

"You're lying," said her father laughing.

Christi looked away. Her father was just teasing her, but lying was exactly what she was planning on doing.

"What's wrong?" asked her father, quick to sense the change in Christi's mood.

"Nothing," said Christi.

"Suddenly you looked so serious."

"Well, it is something," said Christi slowly. "I'm a little nervous. Ms. Cartwright made an announcement after glee club."

"She's dismissing the rest of the club, and she only wants you to sing. The rest of them are going to play the erasers. . . ."

"Daddy," said Christi impatiently.

"Steven, stop teasing her and give her a chance to tell us what's on her mind. What was the announcement?"

Christi told her parents about the chance to try out for the chorus of *Oliver!* with Phil Grey directing, but she didn't tell them that the chorus was supposed to be for boys only.

"Phil Grey!" exclaimed her mother. "I just read today that he was going to direct *Oliver!* I was going to try to get us all tickets. What an opportunity! Honey, that's great."

"Well, I haven't gotten the part yet," said Christi hesitantly.

"As soon as he hears you sing, he'll ask you to star in it," said her father.

Christi shook her head. "No, he's importing professional kids for the leads. He's just using locals for the chorus."

"That's because he hasn't heard you yet," insisted her father.

"Dad," said Christi. "I'm not that good."

"Yes, you are."

"Are you sure you don't mind if I try out?" said Christi. "If I get in the chorus, they'll be having rehearsals for two weeks after school. I probably won't be able to help out at the shop."

"Don't be ridiculous," said her mother. "This sounds like so much fun. Of course you should do it. Don't worry about the shop. We'll survive. When you get rich and famous someday, I don't want to have to read in your autobiography that you had to slave away in the flower shop when you were just a tyke."

"Mom . . ." laughed Christi. She wished her parents weren't being quite so nice about it. It would have been easier to lie to them if they had been meaner.

Chapter 6
Creepy . . . Mean . . . Nasty

Early the next morning, Christi rode her bike to Lizbeth's house. Lizbeth and her brother were shooting baskets in the yard. Max was thirteen, but short for his age. He wasn't even as tall as Lizbeth. He barely nodded to Christi as she rode up, acting as if his sister's friend wasn't worth talking to.

Lizbeth looked up and waved at the same time that she dribbled the ball around Max, made a lay-up and watched it whoosh through the hoop without even touching the rim. Max looked disgusted.

"Good shot," said Christi.

Lizbeth grinned.

"Lucky," muttered Max.

29

"Yeah, well lucky for you, I gotta quit," said Lizbeth. "Christi and I have something important to do before school."

"Yeah, I bet, like talking about how cute *boys* are," teased Max. "Something earth-shattering like that."

"Well, don't worry," said Lizbeth. "We won't talk about you . . . we'll only talk about cute boys."

Christi didn't say anything. The truth was she thought Max was kind of cute. Max played the piano, and he was pretty good. Sometimes when Lizbeth wasn't around he talked to Christi about music, asking what she thought of different groups.

"Come on, Christi," said Lizbeth. They left Max shooting baskets alone in the driveway.

Upstairs in Lizbeth's room, Lizbeth flopped on her canopied bed and looked at Christi critically.

"That's what you're going to wear?" Lizbeth sounded appalled.

Christi looked down at herself. Her jeans were old, and they had a red, heart-shaped bandana on the knee. She was wearing an Ocean Pacific long-sleeved shirt with a sailboat on the back.

"What's wrong?" she asked. "Actually, I think I look pretty unisex already. I'm wearing jeans. Guys wear these shirts, too, and this one is black."

"Look at your feet."

Christi looked down at her lavender, Miss Piggy

sneakers with the satin stripe. "Whoops," she said.

"Squeaky clean lavender sneakers," said Lizbeth. "No way. You need something scuzzy, disgusting-looking."

"Where am I going to get scuzzy sneakers? I don't think there's a store for scuzzy."

"There probably is," said Lizbeth. "But we don't need one. Wait here."

Lizbeth jumped off the bed and left the room, leaving Christi to stare at a life-size poster of Phil Grey that Lizbeth had pasted on her ceiling. He seemed to be looking down at her with a knowing grin, as if telling her that she'd never get away with it.

Lizbeth came back into the room, carrying two scuffed up Nikes in one hand and a pile of what looked like dirty laundry. She threw the pile on the bed and held up the shoes triumphantly.

"How's this for disgusting!" she said. The shoes were worn through on the sides, and they looked as if they had been dipped in dirt.

"Whose are they?"

"Max's. I got all this stuff from him. I should have thought of it earlier. He's the original sleezo in clothes."

"I can't wear Max's clothes. He'll get mad."

"Are you kidding? He doesn't know what's at the bottom of his closet. It's a gold mine in there.

31

He'll never miss this stuff. You can't wear those jeans with the heart on them. They're a dead give away. Wear this instead."

Lizbeth rummaged around on the bed and came up with an old pair of sweatpants and a rugby shirt.

Christi put them on. The pants fit perfectly, and the shirt was just a little bit too big, but the stripes made Christi's shoulders look a little broader.

"See," said Lizbeth approvingly. "With the sweatpants on, nobody can tell that you're not a boy, and *you* don't have to worry about boobs."

"Thanks," said Christi sarcastically. She put on the sneakers. They were a size and a half too big.

"I'll never be able to dance in these," worried Christi. She did a tap dance step and almost fell on her face.

"Don't worry. We'll stuff them with socks," Lizbeth looked at Christi critically. "You still look like a girl. Are you willing to cut your hair?"

Christi looked at her already fairly short hair. "I thought it was short."

"It's short for a girl, but I think it should be shorter. I'll get scissors."

Christi looked at herself in the mirror. "Lizbeth, what do you know about cutting hair?"

"I'm very artistic," said Lizbeth.

"I know, but . . ."

"Look, you can't do this half way."

Christi sighed. "Anything for art."

"That's the spirit. Come on, in the bathroom."

Christi sat on the edge of the bathtub while she watched snippets of her hair fall onto her lap. She couldn't believe Lizbeth had found that much hair to cut. Lizbeth wouldn't let her look at herself until she was done.

"There," said Lizbeth, triumphantly. Christi turned and looked at herself in the mirror. Her hair was less than an inch long. It stuck up from her head at odd angles.

"It looks awful."

"It doesn't," said Lizbeth. "You know, it's kind of cute."

"What am I gonna tell my parents?" wailed Christi.

"Tell them . . . it's punk. Tell them it's the latest style."

"My mom's gonna kill me. She thought it was too short already."

"You look like a boy who's got style. However, now I've got the final touch."

Christi couldn't stop looking at herself in the mirror. She ran her hands through what was left of her hair. It took only a microsecond because there was so little hair left.

Lizbeth came back holding something behind her back. "What's the final touch?" Christi asked dubiously.

"Your glasses, sir," said Lizbeth. She handed Christi a pair of horn-rimmed glasses. "Don't worry, they're just plain glasses. They're left over from an old Halloween costume. Max went as Clark Kent. Some disguise, nobody knew who he was supposed to be. You don't connect Max with Superman exactly."

"I remember that year. He wore a Superman shirt underneath but only he knew he had it on. I thought it was a neat costume . . . funny."

Lizbeth raised her eyebrows. "Considering that you went as a baked potato one year. . . . Anyhow, try on the glasses."

Christi put on the glasses and flung her hands out wide. She looked at herself in the mirror and giggled. She certainly looked different.

"Nearly perfect," said Lizbeth. "One last finishing touch." She brought out an old New York Mets baseball cap, and popped it on Christi's head at an angle.

Christi started to giggle. She couldn't stop. Lizbeth giggled, too. She clapped her hands. "We did it! Ladies and gentlemen, introducing the newest boy in town. . . ."

Christi bowed. "Thank you, thank you. I'd like to introduce myself. Chris . . ." Christi lowered her voice. "Chris Bayton!" She made a face in the mirror. "This is crazy!"

"It's not," insisted Lizbeth. "You really look like a boy. Now you gotta concentrate on the other stuff. You gotta walk like a boy. Think slouch. Watch me." Lizbeth got up. She stuck her hands in her pockets and slunk across the room.

Christi followed her, walking on the balls of her feet so that she bounced just a little bit. She took longer strides than she normally did.

"That's it," cried Lizbeth. "Walk like you own the world."

Christi strode back and forth across the room, playfully pushing Lizbeth aside. "Out of my way, girlie," Christi growled.

Lizbeth laughed. "You've got it. Just think creepy, mean, nasty thoughts and you'll have being a boy down perfectly."

"Creepy . . . mean . . . nasty," repeated Christi. "I think I can get into that."

Chapter 7
You Float.
I Sink.

"Hey, Christi! What a wild haircut!" exclaimed Melody on the way to gym. "I never thought of you as going in for punk. It looks great. Are you thinking of streaking it purple?"

Christi automatically lifted her hand to her head.

Christi giggled. "Well, uh . . . I just wanted to try it."

"It looks *fantastic!* But you should wear some earrings with it. Don't you have pierced ears?"

Christi shook her head. Melody had never paid much attention to her before.

"Say listen," said Melody, drawing Christi aside, so that she was separated from Lizbeth. "I'm

36

having a few kids over tonight. I'd like you to come."

Christi glanced back at Lizbeth who was trying to look as if she didn't feel left out. But Christi knew better.

"We're going to watch MTV all night," said Melody. "My mom only lets me watch it on Friday nights, but we can vote on the video fights. JoAnne and I do it every Friday night."

"I can't tonight," said Christi. "I've got . . ." Christi closed her mouth. She forgot that the audition was now a secret. No one except Lizbeth could know that she was trying out.

Melody saw Christi glancing at Lizbeth. "If you want, you can bring her. I just don't know her very well."

You don't know me well either, Christi thought to herself. It was amazing how people seemed to think her personality had changed just because of a haircut.

"I really can't come, Melody, but thanks for asking me."

Melody shrugged her shoulders as if to say that it was Christi's loss.

Christi shook her head as she watched her go. Lizbeth came up to her side. "What did *she* want?"

"The name of my hairdresser," said Christi.

Lizbeth laughed, but her laugh was just a little bit too loud.

"She liked my new punk haircut," said Christi. "But she thought I should pierce my ears so that I could wear those new metallic earrings."

"I'm thinking of gettting *my* ears pierced," said Lizbeth.

Christi stared at her. "You're kidding!"

"Don't look so shocked. You're not the only one who can change her looks."

"Yeah, but I'm doing it for a purpose."

"Well, so am I. I think pierced ears will make me more sophisticated."

"What does your mom say?"

"She told me that I had to wait until I was twelve. Well, I'm twelve."

"I know, but aren't you scared? Won't it hurt?"

Lizbeth rubbed her ears. "I heard they have a gun with a needle. It's not supposed to hurt at all. Will you go with me?"

"Of course, Lizbeth . . . but . . ."

"But what?"

"I don't know. It makes me feel creepy. It's like mutilating your body."

"It is not!" exclaimed Lizbeth. "And just think of the beautiful earrings I'll be able to wear."

Christi nodded, but she wondered why Lizbeth had chosen that moment to announce that she was getting her ears pierced. Did she think that pierced ears would get her into Melody's crowd? Did she even *want* to be friends with Melody?

38

"Let's go," said Christi. "We're going to be late for gym."

In the locker room, Christi got more comments on her hair. This time, they weren't all compliments.

"What happened?" asked Susannah. "You look like you were scalped."

"It's just a haircut," mumbled Christi.

"Yeah, but it isn't you," said Susannah.

It is me, Christi thought to herself. Very strange indeed how people seemed to think she was different just because her hair was different.

Out on the gym floor, Ms. Levick blew her whistle. "We're going to practice on the parallel bars today," she said.

Christi groaned. Her arms were the weakest part of her body, and she always had trouble on the parallel bars.

Christi watched as Lizbeth swung effortlessly. Lizbeth was so graceful. She made it seem as if the exercise weren't even work, but Christi could see the sweat on her face. The veins on her biceps stood out as she balanced in a perfect handstand on top of the bar.

"Look at her," whispered Melody. "Her arms look like boys' arms."

"She's terrific!" snapped Christi, whirling around.

Melody giggled. "Sorry, I was just giving my opinion."

"Forget it," said Christi, turning back to watch Lizbeth.

Ms. Levick blew her whistle. "Let's have it quiet," she yelled. "Melody, it's your turn after Lizbeth. What's all this talking about?"

"Nothing, Ms. Levick," said Melody sweetly. "I was just complimenting Christi on her new haircut."

Ms. Levick laughed. "Oh, yeah, Christi . . . I couldn't help noticing it. It's uh . . . very short. Do you think it will help you with your gymnastics?"

Not again, Christi thought. Was this going to go on all day? Was it worth it? Several girls in the gym started to laugh.

Lizbeth did a somersault pike dismount. Ms. Levick nodded her head approvingly. "Fantastic, Lizbeth. You've got real talent. I want to keep working with you."

Lizbeth grinned. Melody stepped up to the bars. She needed help for her approach. Lizbeth got a towel and wiped her face. She came and stood next to Christi.

"What's going on between you and Melody?" she said. "I thought she was your new friend."

"Some friend," muttered Christi. "Come on, give me some pointers. It's my turn next."

"Just pretend that the bars can help you fly,"

said Lizbeth. "Think of yourself as floating around them."

"You float," said Christi. "I sink."

Lizbeth laughed. "Okay, just think about tonight. You're going to meet Phil Grey. He's going to think you're sensational, and you're going to get the part."

"Just like that, huh?"

Lizbeth nodded her head. "Just as easy as flying around the parallel bars."

Christi sighed. "That's what I'm afraid of. As I said, I don't fly around the parallel bars. I sink. What if I sink tonight?"

"You won't," promised Lizbeth.

Chapter 8
All Right!

The same woman who had kicked Christi out yesterday was standing guard by the backstage door. Christi adjusted her baseball cap down low over her eyes. "Slouch, slouch," she reminded herself as she walked up to the woman.

"Are you here for the audition?" the woman asked.

Christi nodded.

"Sign in." The woman handed her a clipboard. "We're auditioning in groups of three."

Christi took the pencil and, with a shaking hand, signed Chris Bayton, her new name.

The woman pointed to a backstage area of the theater, letting her in without a second glance. She hadn't recognized her! She had passed!

42

Christi saw a small group of boys lined up in the wings. She went and stood next to them. Several of the boys eyed her. For a second, Christi was scared that one of them had noticed that she was a girl. Then she realized they were just nervous.

She looked around. She was afraid that somebody from school might recognize her, but all the boys were strangers. Suddenly Christi stopped worrying about whether she could pass for a boy and wondered whether she would be good enough. She bit her lip nervously.

The boy standing next to her was chewing his thumbnail. "We only get about sixty seconds out there," he said. "How can they make up their minds in sixty seconds? Phil Grey should give us more time."

"Are you sure he's out there?" Christi asked, her voice rising into a squeak. She coughed to cover up.

The boy looked at her oddly. "Yeah, he's out there, right on stage. Big deal."

"Yeah, big deal," echoed Christi in a low voice, trying to keep her voice cool. Phil Grey would be deciding whether she was good enough or not. Christi prayed that she would be. She reminded herself of all the times she had sung in front of people before. Who cared how she was dressed? She still had the same voice. She was the same person inside, and that person had always been good on stage.

Finally, Christi heard her name called. She raced out from the wings, feeling awkward in Lizbeth's brother's shoes. She came to a lurching stop. Phil Grey was leaning against the piano, staring at her. He looked strange in real life, his skin color looked too pale, as if he were never out in the sun, but it was definitely Phil Grey. The straight, thick black hair. The long legs. The blue eyes.

Two other boys came on stage from the other wing. Phil Grey's assistant handed him a clipboard. "Thanks, Wendie," he said. He looked at the list.

"Chris Bayton?"

"He's here," mumbled Christi. She blinked. "I'm him . . . I mean. . . . I'm here." Her voice cracked as she spoke.

Phil Grey didn't look up. He read the next names on his list. "Danny Liebman and Tony DiSpirito."

Christi almost fell over. Tony DiSpirito! She couldn't believe her lousy luck. Tony was sure to recognize her, and she'd be kicked off the stage before she even had a chance. Christi moved as far downstage as she could so that Tony wouldn't be able to see her face.

"Uh. . . . excuse me," said Phil Grey. "We're

casting for the chorus here, not the star. Chris would you please stay in line. All right, the song I want you to sing is, 'I'd Do Anything for You.' Hit it . . . five, six, seven, eight." He snapped his fingers with each beat.

Christi knew the song well. She sang on key, but Danny, the boy standing next to her, was off by half a tone. She could hear Tony's voice on the other side of Danny also struggling to keep on pitch. Together, Christi and Tony were able to drown out Danny. Christi sang for all she was worth. She could feel sweat on her chest and under her arm as she and Tony sang in perfect unison, as if they had been practicing together for a month.

Just as they were getting to the chorus, at a signal from Phil Grey the piano player stopped abruptly. Christi and Tony kept singing for a few notes. Then out of the corner of her eye, Christi saw Phil Grey bring his finger under his throat and make a cutting motion. Christi stopped in midnote. He must have thought they were awful.

Phil Grey stopped center stage. "Very nice, guys, thank you. Will you just step back with the others. I'll make my decision in a few minutes. You three are the last. . . ." Christi heard him mutter under his breath, "Thank God."

She stepped to the back of the stage, trying to stay as far away from Tony DiSpirito as she could.

Unfortunately, Tony was determined to talk to her.

"You and I were pretty good out there," said Tony.

Christi pulled her baseball cap lower on her head. She grunted something undecipherable, but Tony seemed to accept that as conversation.

"We were much better than that other kid," he whispered.

Christi grunted again. She wondered how long she could get away with just grunts.

Tony studied her. "Do you go to Jefferson?" he asked.

Christi shook her head no. She was beginning to get into the fact that acting like a boy, she could get away without words.

"You sure look like someone I've seen. . . ." said Tony, but before he could finish, Phil Grey interrupted.

He held the clipboard in front of him. He had on a pair of glasses that made him look funny. In his movies, Phil Grey never wore glasses.

He read from the clipboard. "Chris Bayton . . . Tony DiSpirito. You two are the final members of the urchin chorus! Congratulations!"

Christi was so excited that she jumped up and down, letting out a high pitch squeal!

"All right!" cried Tony, giving her a hearty slug on the arm.

His blow sent Christi sprawling across the stage. She rubbed her arm and grinned at Tony. She'd have to remember that guys liked to punch each other when they were happy. At least Tony had saved her from acting just like an excited little girl. For that she was grateful.

Chapter 9
Not Much Hair Left to Cut

As soon as Christi got home, she went up to her room and got out of Max's clothes. She looked at herself in the mirror. She tried to fluff up her hair, but there wasn't much to fluff. She put on her own jeans and shirt, and looked at herself in the mirror. She smiled. When she smiled she looked much more like herself. Then she tried scowling. She looked more like a boy. Then she smiled again, and tossed her head back and forth.

"Christi!"

Startled, Christi twirled around to see her mother staring at her.

"I didn't see you there," said Christi guiltily. Her mother stepped into Christi's room. She lifted her hands towards Christi's head and then dropped them to her side. "Honey, what happened to your hair?"

"Uhh . . . nothing. Lizbeth cut it for me."

"Nothing. It looks like you had an accident and had to have it shaved off."

"Mom!" protested Christi. "It's not that bad. It's the newest style."

Her mother sank down on the bed. "But your red hair is so pretty. It's your best asset. This looks terrible."

"Thanks," mumbled Christi.

"I'm sorry, honey, but it does. How could you just let Lizbeth butcher it!"

"She didn't butcher it. This is very fashionable. It's punk."

"It's awful!"

"Well, Phil Grey didn't think so. I got the part!"

Her mother stood up. "You did!"

Christi nodded. Her mother hugged her. "That's wonderful. I'm sorry I went on so about your hair. After all, it's your hair, and it'll grow back. Come on, let's go down and tell your father."

Mr. Bay was in the middle of making a stew. He stopped browning the meat and stared at Christi.

"What happened to you?" he asked.

"Forget about her hair," said Mrs. Bay. "Christi got into *Oliver!* with Phil Grey."

Her father moved away from the stove. "How

can I forget about her hair, look at it!"

Christi put her hands on her head. "Will you care that I got the part?"

Her father looked embarrassed. "Well, I knew they'd take you!"

Christi was annoyed. "You didn't know! This wasn't just some school thing. There were kids competing from all over town."

"And you made it. I'm surprised that they took you with that haircut though."

Christi put her hands on her head. "Will you stop talking about my hair, please? There is more to me than a haircut."

Her parents looked at each other guiltily. "I'm sorry, Christi," said her father. "But it's a shock. I wish you had asked us before you got it hacked off. I suppose we should be grateful you don't want to die it purple."

"It'll grow back," said Christi softly.

"Thank goodness for that," said her father. "Anyhow, I am extremely proud of you that you got the part. All I'm saying is that I knew it."

"Don't tease her," said her mother. "I think it's fabulous. I can't wait to see you. Have you met Phil Grey yet?"

"Oh, Mom, he's really nice. He's very businesslike, even if he was wearing jeans . . . but you know, he doesn't fool around. And he wears glasses."

"Phil Grey wears glasses? Quick, I'm going to call *People* magazine," joked her father. "It's an exclusive."

Christi laughed. "Daddy . . . it's not funny." But she was grateful that they had finally gotten off the subject of her hair.

"Does he have as nice a smile off screen as he does on?" asked her mother.

"Yeah . . ." said Christi.

Christi's mother sighed. "I think I'm about to turn into a backstage mother. You wouldn't mind, would you, Christi?"

Christi's stomach tightened. She knew her mother was only teasing, but it made her nervous. She would have to be careful to never let her parents come backstage and meet anyone connected with the play.

"Hey, I'm only kidding," said her mother. "You got such a stricken look. I promise I won't do anything to embarrass you."

"And neither will I," said her father. "I won't even call the reporters about Phil Grey's glasses. Besides, I don't want to see a picture of you in the paper until your hair grows a little."

Christi tried to laugh, but she felt worried. "Actually, Phil Grey isn't letting anyone in to watch rehearsals, parents or reporters," she said, relieved for once to be telling the truth. He *had* announced that rehearsals would be closed. He didn't want anyone watching him directing for the first time.

"Well, we're allowed to come to the performance, aren't we?" asked her father.

"Sure," said Christi. She blinked her eyes, something she always did when she was nervous. What would she tell her parents when they saw that the program read Chris Bayton instead of Christine Bay. Well, Lizbeth would help her think of something. She'd just have to tell her parents it was a typo. Programs were always full of typos.

Christi sat at the dining-room table, wishing that she could talk to Lizbeth. As soon as dinner was over, she ran to the phone to call her.

"Did you get the part?" Lizbeth asked excitedly.

"I did!" squealed Christi.

"Wait. You've got to tell me all about it in person. Come over this minute."

"We're just finishing dinner," said Christi.

"How can you be hungry on the same day that you actually met Phil Grey?"

Christi laughed. "I'll ask my parents if I can come over." Christi put her hand over the receiver. "Mom and Dad, it's Lizbeth. Can I go over there? I'm finished with dinner."

Mr. and Mrs. Bay looked at each other. "Sure," said her mother. "Just clear your plate. I can tell you're too excited to sit still."

Christi hung up the phone, a big smile on her face.

"Just make sure Lizbeth stays away from the scissors," warned her father. "There's not much left to cut."

Chapter 10

What a Jerk!
What a Riot!

Lizbeth answered the doorbell practically before it rang. She must have been waiting just inside. Her eyes were bright with excitement. She gave Christi a hug, practically lifting her off the ground.

"What happened?" asked Max who was playing a great Ray Charles blues song on the piano in the living room.

"Nothing," said Lizbeth, winking at Christi.

"Nothing. You two always greet each other like that? Very cute."

"I . . ." Christi started to tell Max that she had gotten the part, then she realized she couldn't. Max gave her a curious look.

"Don't mind him, he's just a boy," said Lizbeth. "Come on." As they climbed the stairs to Lizbeth's room, Christi heard Max play a Stevie Wonder song. He was really good. She almost wished she could stay and sing with him, but she followed Lizbeth up to her room.

Lizbeth closed the door to her room. "Okay . . . tell me *everything!*"

"Well, it was a riot. My disguise worked perfectly. Remember that woman at the door who threw us out; she just let me waltz through. I was one of the last three to audition, and guess who was in my group? You'll never guess."

Lizbeth shook her head. "Don't make me guess. Come on, I want to hear about Phil Grey."

"Okay, it was Tony DiSpirito!"

Lizbeth shrieked. "Tony was there and he saw you?"

"Yup," said Christi, feeling excited just retelling it. "He never even guessed who I was." She started laughing at the memory of it.

"What a jerk!" cried Lizbeth. "What a riot!"

"Oh, it was. We sang together. Actually he and I were pretty good. We were the last two picked. The other guy who tried out with us didn't make it."

"And Phil Grey actually spoke to you?"

"He did, he spoke my name . . . or rather my fake name."

"Don't think of it as a fake name, think of it as your stage name."

"Lizbeth, you somehow make it all seem so simple."

"It is."

Christi flopped down on the bed. "I don't think it's going to be simple at all. For example, what about your brother? I can't wear the same clothes all week to rehearsal. I'll have to change. Even boys don't wear the same thing every day. Won't your brother notice when all his clothes start disappearing?"

"Don't worry," said Lizbeth. "I have it completely figured out. I'll come home after school every day and get another Chris Bayton outfit out of Max's closet. Then I'll bring it back right after you're finished with it. With his closet we could borrow things for a month and he'd never notice."

"I just wish his feet weren't a size and a half bigger than mine," groaned Christi. "I'm going to trip right in the middle of a dance."

"That's okay. Boys are supposed to have big clumsy feet," said Lizbeth. "It will make you all the more authentic."

Christi frowned at the word authentic. "I just wish I didn't have to lie so much."

"It's not such a big lie," said Lizbeth.

"I know. But I felt bad talking to my parents

tonight. And now it's going to get even more complicated. Maybe I should tell them the truth."

"Definitely not," said Lizbeth. "They might tell you that you can't do it, and then you'd lose your chance to work with Phil Grey. You don't want that, do you?"

"No," admitted Christi. "Oh, Lizbeth, I wish you could have been there. He's so cute. He really is. Only he's sort of serious when he works. He even wears glasses."

"Phil Grey wears glasses!"

Christi nodded. "I was glad you got me glasses as part of my disguise. It gave us something in common. Maybe he picked me because of my glasses."

"He picked you because you were good," insisted Lizbeth. "And don't you forget it."

"He picked me because he thought I was a boy," said Christi. "That's what I can't forget."

Chapter 11
Girls Are Dumb

On Monday, Christi could hardly concentrate knowing that she had rehearsal that afternoon. She doodled Phil Grey's name in her notebook, putting a heart around it. Then she stared at what she had drawn. It seemed very unprofessional of her. Quickly she scratched it out.

"Christi?" asked Mr. Vickers, her teacher. "Am I disturbing you by asking you a question? Didn't you hear me call your name?"

"I'm sorry, Mr. Vickers. I didn't."

"I hope you didn't lose some of your brains with that haircut," said Mr. Vickers. "It's not like you to daydream during class."

Christi felt herself blush. She heard Melody

and JoAnne's loud laugh from the back of the class.

To her surprise, Mr. Vickers was blushing, too. "I'm sorry Christi. That was unkind of me. However, now that I've got your attention, would you please answer my question. If you remember, we were discussing *Watership Down*. Now . . ."

Somehow Christi forced herself to concentrate. She couldn't wait for school to be over. Finally, the last period bell rang.

"Are you okay?" Lizbeth asked.

Christi nodded. "I'm just nervous. This afternoon is the first day of *real* rehearsal."

"I've got your outfit," whispered Lizbeth. "But from now on, we've got to be very careful." She handed Christi a brown paper bag. Christi looked in. There was another pair of sweatpants and one of Max's alligator shirts.

"Don't look at it here!" hissed Lizbeth. "You'd make a lousy secret agent."

Just then Tony came down the hall, swinging his arms. Christi quickly turned her back on him.

"Very cool," whispered Lizbeth. "Look, we're going to have to figure out a different way for me to pass you Max's clothes. This is too dangerous."

"This is crazy. Maybe I should call the whole thing off."

"*Never!*" shouted Lizbeth.

Several kids turned around.

"Shh," whispered Christi.

"Sorry. Anyhow, you can't quit. You haven't even started. Go on. You'd better get there quickly. You don't want to be late for your first day of rehearsal."

"I wish you could come with me," said Christi.

"So do I," said Lizbeth. "But go on."

Christi whipped into the girls' room and changed into Max's clothes. Lizbeth was convinced that sweatpants were the proper dance outfit for a boy. Christi put on Max's baseball cap. Even with her hair short, she felt safer with her cap on.

Before the rehearsal began, Phil Grey called a meeting of the full urchin chorus. A row of folding chairs was lined up onstage. The members of the chorus took their seats. Christi watched to see where Tony sat, and then took a chair at the opposite end. Phil Grey stood by the piano, running through the arrangements for one of the chorus's songs.

The other kids in the chorus all talked and joked with each other loudly, not paying any attention to Phil. Christi tucked in her shirt. Phil clapped his hands to get everybody's attention. Christi sat bolt upright in her chair, her back straight, her hands folded in her lap, and her ankles neatly crossed. Most of the other boys in the chorus continued laughing and wiggling around in their seats.

"Okay," said Phil. "There are some ground rules I want to get straight right up front." Gradually, the boys stopped laughing and gave him their attention, but they all slouched in their chairs. Christi was the only one sitting up straight, her eyes never leaving Phil Grey's face.

He paced up and down in front of them nervously. "I know that for most of you, outside of school plays, this may be your first production, but I want you to know that I expect the same professionalism from you guys as I do from the other actors."

Christi looked down the line. She realized that she was the only one sitting straight. She studied the boy sitting next to her. He was completely relaxed, arms crossed over his chest, shoulders resting on the back of the chair, hips almost slipping beyond the edge of the seat. She slouched down, crossed her arms over her chest, and cocked her head back against the chair.

She looked up at the ceiling pretending to be bored as she heard Phil say, "I expect you to be on time, know your lines . . . and work hard."

Christi slouched a teeny bit farther, crossing her feet in front of her so that only her heels were on the floor. Unfortunately, the stage floor was slippery. Her heels slipped. She fell off the chair and sprawled on the floor right at Phil's feet.

She was mortified. Clumsily she straightened her glasses and checked to see if her baseball cap was in place.

Phil looked down at her, and started to laugh. "I demand respect. However, I don't expect you to throw yourself at my feet. Mr. . . ?"

Christi struggled to her feet, feeling like she wanted to die. "Chris . . ." she said in a squeaky voice. Then she brought her voice down an octave. "Chris . . . Bay . . . ton."

Phil extended his hand to her. He smiled at her. "Welcome to show business, Chris," he said.

Christi shook his hand up and down, in a trance, forgetting to let go.

Phil smiled at her again, almost laughing. He released her hand. Christi was left with her hand still extended in midair. She lowered it in slow motion, not believing that she had actually touched him.

Phil turned back to the group. "Welcome to all of you. Now let's follow Chris's lead and hit the boards. Places, everyone."

Phil moved through the group, quickly pairing boys off into sets of partners. Christi watched him adoringly. He had turned what could have been the world's worst moment into an easy joke.

He had seen that she had been mortified, and he had been extra nice.

He placed her next to a tall, rather awkward boy with a few pimples on the side of his cheek. "You and Bobby will work together. You are partners. It will be like the buddy system. You'll run lines with each other and help each other with dance routines, and you look out for each other."

Phil looked at Christi critically. "Chris, you're gonna have to lose that hat. Urchins in Oliver Twist's time weren't into baseball."

Christi's hand shot up to her cap. "Uh . . . it's my lucky hat. I'll take it off before the play, I promise."

Phil shook his head. "All right, but don't get too superstitious about it." He moved on down the line.

Christi didn't realize that her new partner was speaking to her. "Excuse me," said Christi politely. "I didn't hear you."

Bobby looked down at his feet as he talked to her. "I said, 'You auditioned with DiSpirito?' "

Christi nodded.

"Whaddya think of him?"

"He's kind of cute," answered Christi without thinking.

Bobby stared at her. Christi felt the blood go to her face.

"You putting me on or what?" asked Bobby.

Christi laughed nervously. "Yeah, sorta, that's what I heard some girl say . . . that *she* thought he was cute. Girls are really dumb, huh."

Christi swallowed hard as Bobby stared at her suspiciously. Christi knew she was going to have to be careful. Boys didn't go around calling each other cute. Not if they didn't want to get punched in the mouth.

Chapter 12

Boys Don't Wear Earrings!

Finally, it was Saturday, and the urchins didn't have rehearsal until two in the afternoon. Christi was looking forward to a morning of sleeping late and doing nothing.

But at nine o'clock, she heard the telephone ring. Her father poked his head in the door. "It's Lizbeth," he said. "I told her you were exhausted, but she said it was an emergency."

Christi jumped out of bed. "Lizbeth, what's wrong?" she asked.

"Today's the day."

Christi shook her head. "What day?"

"The day I'm going to have my ears pierced," said Lizbeth. "Don't you remember? You promised you'd go with me."

Christi groaned to herself. "Today?"

"Well, if you're too busy." Lizbeth sounded hurt. "But you did promise. I told you about it in the beginning of the week."

"I'm sorry. I forgot. So much has been going on this week."

"I know," said Lizbeth. "For *you*."

"Lizbeth, I'm really sorry. Honest. When are you going? I've got rehearsal at two."

"Great. Mom said we can go around eleven, and then she promised to take us out for lunch as a treat. I get to have whatever I want. I think I'll ask to have a hot fudge sundae."

"Aren't you scared?" asked Christi.

"A little. I'm glad you're going to come."

"Me, too. Are you sure you want to go through with it?"

"Of course," said Lizbeth. "We'll pick you up around ten-thirty."

Christi fell back into bed. She felt like pulling the covers up over her head. The last thing she wanted to do was spend her one free morning watching Lizbeth get holes punched in her ears.

Downstairs her father was in the shop straightening out the display in the cooler. "I thought you were going to sleep all morning," he said.

"Lizbeth's getting her ears pierced today. I promised I'd hold her hand."

Her father's eyes widened. "Isn't she young for that?"

"Daddy," protested Christi. "Half the girls in our class have pierced ears."

"Well, you're not having it done today, are you? This isn't something you and Lizbeth cooked up without telling us, is it?"

"Don't be ridiculous. If I was going to do it, I'd tell you and Mom. I wouldn't sneak behind your back." Christi sounded a little too self-righteous, even to her own ears. While it was true she wasn't planning on having her ears pierced, she wasn't exactly being straight with her parents, either.

"You don't have to bite your father's head off," said her mother. "You've been awfully touchy this week. I know you're working hard on the production, but are you sure it's not too much for you?"

"I'm sorry," said Christi. "It's just nerves. We only have one more week of rehearsals and then the performance." Christi looked out the window. To her relief, Lizbeth and her mother drove up. "I've got to go now," she said quickly. She kissed her parents and rushed out the door.

Lizbeth's mother was a tall, beautiful black woman who sometimes took modeling jobs. Christi liked her, but she felt just a little bit intimidated because Mrs. Collins was *so* beautiful.

"Hi, Christi. That's quite a haircut you've got."

"Lizbeth helped me with it."

Mrs. Collins smiled. "Next time come to me."

Lizbeth giggled.

"Do you want to get your ears pierced, too?" Mrs. Collins asked.

"No way," said Christi. "I'm strictly here for moral support."

"Mom says it doesn't hurt, right?" Lizbeth looked over at her mother nervously.

"No, a friend of mine owns a jewelry store. He's done it thousands of times. He has a new machine. It'll be very quick. It's just like a tiny pinprick."

Somehow even the thought of putting holes in her ears gave Christi a stomachache.

The jewelry store was in the middle of the mall on the second floor. As they made their way through the Saturday shoppers, several people stopped and stared at Mrs. Collins. Christi tried to match her long graceful strides. Lizbeth was dressed in a red miniskirt and turquoise tights. She looked very cute. Christi felt dowdy beside them, and she wished she had worn something besides her jeans and a sweatshirt.

At the door to the jewelry store, Lizbeth stopped. Christi took her hand. "It's going to be okay," she whispered. "It's not going to hurt."

Lizbeth gave Christi a weak smile.

The jewelry store owner greeted Mrs. Collins like a long lost friend. "Your daughter," he said, leaning over and taking Lizbeth's cheeks in his hand. "She's as beautiful as you are. Do you want a career in modeling, too?"

Lizbeth giggled. "I'm not as pretty as my mother."

The owner shook his head. "No one's as pretty as your mother," he whispered. "But you have the bones of a beauty. I can tell you're going to be a swan."

He glanced over at Christi as if wondering what such an ugly duckling was doing among the swans.

"This is my friend, Christi Bay," said Lizbeth.

"Are you here to have your ears pierced, too?" he asked.

Christi shook her head anxiously.

The owner examined Lizbeth's earlobes. "They're nice and thin. This is going to be a piece of cake."

He took out a machine that looked like a gun connected to a wire chord. "First, I'll put a little antiseptic on your ears," said the owner.

"When I was about Lizbeth's age," Mrs. Collins said, "my sister held an ice cube on my ear. Then she got my mother's biggest needle and just poked."

"Kids still do it to themselves at slumber parties," said the owner. "I see plenty of ragged holes."

He held the contraption up to Lizbeth's ear. Christi held Lizbeth's hand, but she couldn't look. The gun made a little popping noise, and then a drop of blood appeared on Lizbeth's ear. The owner inserted a solid gold stud.

Lizbeth looked away, but she didn't even flinch as he did the other ear.

"Done," said Mrs. Collins. She kissed Lizbeth on the cheek. "Come look at yourself in the mirror. You look like such a young lady."

Lizbeth moved up to the mirror. She put her hand to the studs.

"No, don't touch," said the owner. "We use solid gold so there won't be any infection, but you have to be careful for a few weeks."

Lizbeth smiled at her image in the mirror. The earrings made her look a little bit older, more sophisticated. "It really didn't hurt," said Lizbeth.

Christi felt a twinge of jealousy. "They look great on you," she said.

"With your hair so short, earrings would look wonderful on you," said Mrs. Collins.

"I can't," said Christi.

"You *really* should," urged Lizbeth. "Do it now!"

"I can't," whispered Christi. "You know why."

Mrs. Collins went to pay the owner for the earrings.

"Come on," said Lizbeth. "Don't be chicken."

"I'm not chicken," whispered Christi urgently. "Boys don't wear earrings."

Lizbeth rolled her eyes. "You're not a boy!"

"I know," said Christi. But she felt confused.

Chapter 13
Check Him Out

Lizbeth and Christi both had hot fudge sundaes for lunch. Then Christi left to go to rehearsal. She felt like a spy leading two lives.

At the Civic Center she slipped into the ladies' room and changed into Max's clothes. She left her own clothes in a shopping bag in the corner of the ladies' room, sneaked out then hurried on stage.

Phil clapped his hands, calling for a run-through of the urchins' dance number. The routine called for the chorus to drop on one hand with their legs extended and do a full circle, pivoting on their hand, almost as if they were break dancing. Phil's idea was that urchins were really street kids. He wanted the energy of today's street kids, but he didn't want it to look too modern.

Christi worked hard to follow the spirit of what he wanted. Finally the routine ended. "Good work, take five," said Phil.

Christi went off to the side to practice the new dance steps. Out of the corner of her eye, Christi saw Tony. He was looking at her curiously, and then she saw that he had gone behind a backdrop to practice his steps. It was as if he didn't want anyone to catch him practicing, that it wasn't cool to practice. But Christi decided she didn't care. She wanted to be as good as she could be, and if the boys thought that was strange, well it was just too bad.

Bobby gave Christi a dirty look. Did he think she was trying too hard? Tony came out from his secret practicing and dashed by her, giving her a jab in the arm as he passed. "Yo, whaddya say, Baytony?"

"About what?" asked Christi seriously. Tony laughed.

Phil overheard them and started chuckling to himself. "You know, Chris. You're a pretty funny guy. A real original talent. I'm impressed. I like the way you worked on the new step during the break. You could have quite an interesting career ahead of you . . . if you keeping working hard."

Christi looked up at him adoringly. "Oh, I will, I will," she said fervently.

Phil cracked up. He slapped her on the back as

he went off backstage. "Terrific! I love it!" He was laughing so hard that he almost had tears in his eyes.

Christi stared after him. She couldn't figure out what she had said that was so funny. He said that she was an "original talent," but what was so original about her? What had she said that was so funny? She knew she looked like a boy, that part had been easy, but Christi was beginning to understand boys acted different, and she was standing out because she didn't act quite like they did. She wasn't sure she wanted to. Working on a show with Phil Grey was an opportunity that came once in a lifetime. Why should she have to act cool about it?

Christi saw Tony and the other urchins standing in a circle.

"Hey," said Steve. "Wanna see something neat?"

"Sure," said Christi. She joined the boys and looked down into Steve's hand. He was holding a small white mouse.

"He's neat, isn't he?" said Steve. "He's my pet. I snuck him in. Want to hold him?"

Christi had always hated to pick up mice. She knew it was a cliché—that girls were scared of mice, but she was. She hated the way their little nails felt on her hand.

"Uhh . . . no thanks," said Christi, swallowing hard. "I gotta do something."

"Suit yourself," said Steve.

Christi left them and went down the hall. She needed to sneak back into the ladies' room to collect her clothes. She looked around carefully to make sure that nobody else was there. She felt so silly having to sneak into the ladies' room, but she had to be careful. If anyone saw her, how could she possibly explain what she was doing in there!

Just as Christi was about to open the door, two actors came down the hall. Christi whirled around and pretended to study the bulletin board intently. Unfortunately, the bulletin board had only one very tiny notice on it—a faded card announcing the union rules for handling props.

Christi didn't know how long she could go on pretending to read the three-line notice. The actors gave her a curious look and passed by her without saying anything.

Christi took one last frantic look around. No one else was there so she jumped swiftly into the ladies' room, pushing the door closed behind her.

She gathered up her clothes and started to sneak back out of the ladies' room. Just as she got the door open she saw Tony leaning against the bulletin board, talking to Bobby and Steve. Christi was about to slam the door shut again when she heard her name mentioned.

"That Bayton guy sure is weird," said Bobby.

"I'm not sure I like having him as a partner."

"Yeah," said Steve. "He's a real snob. He acts like he's too good for us."

"I don't know," said Tony. "He doesn't seem so bad, and he sure can sing and dance."

"Yeah, but he's always browning up to Phil Grey, trying to impress him with how hard he works," said Steve.

"I tell you he's weird," said Bobby. "I should know. I'm his partner. Like he keeps that hat on. Maybe he's a midget in disguise, and he's bald. He sure acts like an old man."

Tony laughed. "I say we check him out and see what his story is."

Christi leaned against the inside of the ladies' room door. "This is definitely not going to be easy," she whispered to herself.

Chapter 14
No More Disguises

The next day when Christi came down to breakfast she felt a little stiff from the new routines. She hobbled over to the refrigerator and poured herself some orange juice.

"Are you all right?" asked her father. "You look like you just ran the marathon on a rainy day."

"You should try rehearsals with Phil Grey," said Christi. "He makes running a marathon look easy."

"Are you going to survive?"

Christi nodded. "I'm tough."

Her father laughed. "You sure don't look tough." Christi was wearing her flowered cotton skirt with an eyelet petticoat that peeked out from under the hem.

"Are you having a party in school today?" her mother asked.

Christi looked down at her outfit. When she had gotten up in the morning, she had just felt like wearing something very feminine.

"No party."

"Well, you look very pretty," said her father.

"Do you have rehearsal this afternoon again?" asked her mother.

"Yeah . . . it's every day this week. I won't be home until about six."

"Do you want one of us to pick you up? You'll be awfully tired. Maybe you shouldn't ride your bike. You know accidents can happen when you're tired."

"No, Mom," said Christi quickly. "Don't bother. We never know exactly when Phil is going to let us go, so I couldn't tell you what time to be there. The best thing is for me to just take my bike. It's still so hot out, and it stays light until later anyhow."

"I know," said her father. "We're having one of the hottest Septembers I can remember. It's bad for business, though. Everybody's garden still looks beautiful."

"Relax," said Mrs. Bay. "Enjoy the hot weather. It will be gone soon enough, and then we'll be complaining that nobody ever goes out because it's too cold. Besides, when Christi becomes rich and famous, we can retire. We can just bask in the glory."

Christi felt embarrassed. There wasn't going to be much glory if she stayed in the chorus disguised as a boy.

"Hey, we're just kidding," said her father.

Christi knew that he was, but it still bothered her. She felt vaguely uneasy, and the feeling didn't quite go away all day.

In school, Lizbeth showed off her new earrings to all their classmates. "Did it hurt when you slept?" asked JoAnne.

"Not a bit," said Lizbeth proudly.

"Let me see," said Melody. She examined Lizbeth's ears. "It's a good job. At least the holes are even. The bozo who did mine made the hole on my left ear about a quarter of an inch lower than my right. See."

Melody stuck her face close to Lizbeth's. Then she gave Lizbeth advice on how to avoid getting an infection. Christi felt left out.

Suddenly, Melody and Lizbeth seemed to have a lot in common, and Christi couldn't think of anything to add to the conversation. She tried to get Lizbeth alone in the lunchroom. "Did you bring my new clothes to wear this afternoon?" Christi asked.

"Shhh . . ." said Lizbeth. "You'd make a lousy spy. I told you not to talk about it here. I'll meet you by the bus stop at three."

"Lizbeth, why can't you just slip me the clothes here in the lunchroom?"

"Are you kidding?" exclaimed Lizbeth. "Suppose my brother happened to find you carrying his smelly shirts. It would be all over. No, do it my way."

"Okay."

Lizbeth stared at her. "For someone who is getting to spend every afternoon this week with Phil Grey, you don't look very cheery."

Christi looked around the lunchroom worried that someone would overhear them talking about Phil Grey.

"Hey, you two, come on over here," shouted Melody, pointing to two extra seats at her table.

"You seem to have a new friend."

"She was your friend last week. She's not so bad. Anyhow, what are you so depressed about?"

"I can't talk about it now," whispered Christi.

"See," said Lizbeth triumphantly. "We need secrecy in carrying out this mission."

Christi laughed. "Somehow, you always make me feel better," she told Lizbeth.

"I do?" said Lizbeth surprised. "Why?"

Christi shrugged. "It's a secret," she whispered.

At three o'clock after school, Christi looked around for Lizbeth, but she couldn't find her anywhere. Then she remembered, and rode her bike to the appointed bus stop, two blocks away from the Civic Center.

Lizbeth was seated on the bench at the stop disguised in an oversized trenchcoat, a floppy hat, and dark glasses. She was holding a magazine in front of her nose, but clearly she wasn't reading it. Every few seconds she looked furtively from side to side like a spy in a cartoon. Between her feet, she held a backpack full of clothes.

Christi rode up on her bicycle. She couldn't believe her eyes.

"Ps-s-sst . . . Christi," whispered Lizbeth.

Christi stared at her friend. "Lizbeth? What are you doing in that dumb coat. It's a million degrees out here."

Lizbeth looked offended. "It's a disguise. I'm wearing a disguise so that nobody recognizes me while I'm giving you your disguise."

Lizbeth whipped the magazine up again in front of her face. Very stealthily she used her feet to slide the backpack towards Christi.

"Lizbeth, we *can* be seen together. We have been for years. It's the guys in the chorus we have to fool. Not total strangers."

Just then Melody rode by on her bicycle. "Hi,

Lizbeth," she waved. "Love your outfit."

Lizbeth flung her magazine down in disgust. "Phooey!" she cried.

Christi was laughing so hard she couldn't stop.

"It's not funny," said Lizbeth, but she was laughing herself.

"Don't worry," said Christi. "Knowing you, you'll come up with a better disguise soon."

"I worked really hard on this one," said Lizbeth, shrugging her way out of the raincoat. "Well, you'd better take the clothes and get changed. You don't want to be late for rehearsal."

"Thanks," said Christi, finally able to stop laughing. "I needed a good laugh."

"Here," said Lizbeth. "The magazine's part of your disguise. It's *Motocross*. I stole it from Max. All the guys read it. I don't know why. None of them have motorcycles."

Christi stuck the magazine in her back pocket. "Boys do a lot of things I don't understand. But thanks for the magazine. It's a great touch."

Lizbeth nodded, but she looked preoccupied. "I've got to work on my own disguise," she said.

Christi laughed. Then she stopped. She realized Lizbeth was serious.

"Is Max getting suspicious?" she asked.

"No," said Lizbeth. "But I'm getting sick of being on the outside while you get all the fun. I'm working on a disguise that will get *me* backstage, too. I want to meet Phil Grey, too. You get all the glory, and I get all the work."

"It's not so much glory," said Christi. "But you're right. It's not fair. I'll find a way to introduce you to Phil Grey. But promise me, Lizbeth, no more disguises."

"I can't promise *that!*" exclaimed Lizbeth.

Christi worried about exactly what Lizbeth would do next.

Chapter 15
Relax! That's an Order!

Christi was out of breath. She had just two minutes before the rehearsal began. Wendie called the chorus on stage. Christi ran to her place. She waited impatiently for her partner, Bobby, to join her. Bobby shambled on stage, looking like he had just come off a soccer field.

"You were almost late," whispered Christi.

"Cool your jets, Chris," snapped Bobby. "I'm here in plenty of time."

They went through the new routine. Christi felt that they were slightly off. She wished Bobby had been willing to work just a little harder with her, maybe even practice alone with her, but every time she had asked him, Bobby had refused.

Phil surveyed the chorus line critically. He

pulled on his ear; Christi noticed that he did that whenever he was thinking.

Then he cleared his throat. "Before we run through that number again, I want to make one quick change. Bobby, you team up with Jason, and Chris, you and Tony are partners. I think the staging will work better."

Chris stared down the line at Tony. What a disaster! She couldn't work with him as her partner. He'd guess who she was! Christi had been avoiding Tony at each rehearsal, trying to put as much space between them as possible. Now Phil Grey was insisting they work side by side. This was terrible!

Bobby dutifully trotted over to Jason, giving Christi a glance as if he was glad to get rid of her. Christi panicked. She had to do something. She couldn't let Tony be her partner.

"No! It won't work!" she said in a loud, demanding voice.

Phil turned, clearly surprised at her tone. "Chris, just relax and keep doing what you do best, which is acting and dancing. Let me take care of the directing, okay?"

Tony moved across stage and stood next to her, giving her a cocky look. Christi pushed her basball cap even farther down on her eyes and stared at the floor.

Phil turned to the pianist, "All right . . . take

it from the top, and step up the tempo just a bit."

Christi tried to dance as far away from Tony as possible. She kept her eyes on the floor. She danced clumsily, stumbling so badly that she almost ended up on the floor.

She tried to pull herself together, but the more she tried, the more she seemed to fall apart. Finally Phil clapped his hands, but it was an angry, short clap. "Stop, stop! Chris, what's wrong with you? You know this routine."

"It's my shoes," Christi stammered. "They're a little loose."

"What are you doing in loose shoes?" snapped Phil angrily.

Tony took a step forward. "Maybe it's my fault. I'm used to dancing with my old partner. I think I'm throwing Chris off."

Christi looked at him with surprise. Tony knew she was dancing like a clutz. If anything, he had tried to help her in the routine, slowing himself down so that they'd both look better.

Phil frowned. He pulled at his ear. "No excuses. I'm counting on you guys to roll with the punches. I picked up the beat, but you'll dance at that speed when we open, so you'd better get used to picking up your feet. All right, that's it today. See you guys tomorrow . . . on time and ready to work." He paused. "Chris, can I talk to you for a minute?"

Christi crossed over to him, dragging her feet. She wondered if he was going to fire her. First she had talked back to him, and then she had stumbled all over the stage. She couldn't blame him if he did want to get rid of her.

She stood in front of him as if waiting for her execution. Phil put his arm around her shoulder. "Come on off stage with me a minute," he said, steering her down the steps of the stage, towards the empty chairs in the audience.

Christi kept her head down, determined not to cry, no matter what happened. Phil Grey would not see her cry.

They sat down in the back. It was strange to sit on a dusty seat, and look up at the stage.

Phil stuck his feet up on the chair in front of him. "I love sitting in an empty theater like this. Always makes me feel like I'm one of the privileged few."

Christi nodded. She swallowed hard. "I'm sorry I messed up before," she said very quietly.

"That's what I wanted to talk to you about," said Phil. "You know, Chris, when I was your age, I wanted more than anything in the world to be a great actor. And there were a couple of times when I blew it by trying too hard. I don't want to see you make the same mistake. You've got a lot of talent and a lot of time to develop it. I want you to *promise* me not to push too hard."

Christi stared at him. Wasn't he going to yell at her?

Phil laughed. "I love that eager look on your face. I mean it, Chris, you've got real talent, it's just that you're too intense. Now come on, I asked you to promise me something, remember?"

"To promise not to try too hard?"

"That's right. It shouldn't be too difficult. Take your cue from Tony and some of the other guys. Just relax—that's an order."

"Sure," mumbled Christi, thinking that she'd have to be careful about relaxing *too* much around Tony.

"Atta boy," said Phil, giving her a tap on the shoulder as he got up. "I'll see you tomorrow. And no more clumsy feet, right? Get some shoes that fit right!"

"Right," said Christi, looking down at Max's oversized Nikes. She would do anything, she realized, to have her own shoes back—how could she relax when she always had to wear someone else's shoes!

Chapter 16
High Score

Christi was surprised to see Tony and some of the other guys waiting for her when she got backstage. Tony took her aside. "Did you get in trouble?" he asked.

Christi shook her head. "Nah, he just wants me not to be so uptight. Thanks for covering for me."

"No sweat. We're partners now, man. We look out for each other." He punched her good-naturedly on the arm. Christi hesitated for a minute and then gave him a tentative rabbit punch, feeling a little silly as she did it, silly but good. She wondered why boys spend so much time punching each other.

Just then, Bobby and a group of guys from the chorus came up to Tony. They eyed Christi suspiciously. "Hey, Tony," said Bobby, "Anderson says he's gonna burn your high score at the arcade this afternoon."

"Oh yeah, Anderson?"

Jason answered, "Yeah, DiSpirito. I'm about to make you video game history."

Without waiting to see if Christi would come with them, the boys took off. Christi realized how much of an outsider she was. She had been so self-involved worrying about her disguise and about Phil Grey that she hadn't noticed that she really hadn't made any friends. She felt a little wistful as she watched them take off.

Then Tony turned around. "Hey, man," he said.

Christi didn't realize he was talking to her.

"Hey, Chris. You play video games, don't you?"

Bobby grabbed Tony's arm. Christi could hear him whisper, "Hey, don't ask him."

"You *do* play, don't you?" repeated Tony, shaking off Bobby's arm.

Christi nodded.

"Well then, come with us?" said Tony. He winked at Bobby. "We could get to know you better."

Christi felt trapped. She remembered overhearing Tony saying that they should check her out. She knew she was being tested but then, on the other hand, they had picked just the right place to test her.

90

"Sure," said Christi. "I'll come."

Outside they got on their bikes. Christi was grateful now that her parents had made her get a boy's bike. But what should she do about her helmet? Would the guys think she was sissy for wearing one?

"What're you waiting for?" asked Tony. Christi was relieved to see him take a helmet out of his knapsack and shove it on his head. "Let's go." Tony took off, executing an expert wheelie as he went, riding along on his back wheel, perfectly balanced up in the air.

Christi pushed her weight back on her seat and tried to lift the front half of her bike with her hands. The front wheels came off about three inches and then back down again with a thud, almost throwing her off the bike.

Bobby looked at her suspiciously. She tried again. This time she found the right fulcrum of balance, and her bike stayed perched on one wheel for several seconds. She felt elated. Up ahead, she saw Tony and the others race around the corner. She biked furiously to keep up with them, putting her bike in its highest gear so that she used all her strength with each cycle.

She loved the feeling of going that fast. Just as she rounded the corner, Lizbeth stepped off the curb with her mother. Christi whipped by them, giving them a jaunty little wave. "Yo, Lizbeth," she cried. She tried a wheelie again. This time it was a piece of cake. She pushed her front wheel way up in the air until she was practically perpendicular to the ground. She felt as if she could stay up on one wheel forever.

Then suddenly her rear wheel caught on a piece of gravel, and Christi wavered in the air for a moment and then went tumbling down, landing with her bike on top of her. Tony looked back and laughed, but he rode over. "Are you okay?" he asked.

Christi stood up, a little shaken. "Sure," she said. She pulled her bike back up. Everything looked okay. She gave Lizbeth a sheepish shrug. "See you," she whispered.

Then she raced after the other boys. Soon she caught up to them, and then she passed everyone except Tony. By the time they got to the mall, Christi was the leader.

Christi's face was red from the wind. She swung her leg over the crossbar, chained her bike up and waited for the others. Tony was only seconds behind, but the others were strung out behind him.

"You always ride that fast?" Tony asked.

"It felt good," said Christi. "I guess I was still uptight after Phil talked to me. I just liked feeling free. Don't you feel sometimes like you just want to cut loose?"

"Yeah," said Tony doubtfully.

Suddenly Christi's elation left her. She wondered if she had talked too much. Did boys think you had to just make jokes or else not talk at all?

She sighed as they walked into the arcade. She was bored with video games. When they had first come out, she had discovered an unexpected talent for them. Her mother told her that it wasn't surprising. When she was a little baby, she had shocked everyone by how quickly she had learned to manipulate her toys. "You were a whizz at the busy box," said her mother. "If you ask me, these games are just busy boxes for older kids." Her mother was a flop at video games.

"Want to play?" Tony asked.

Christi pulled on her ear, not realizing she was unconsciously copying Phil.

"Okay," she stepped up.

"Hey, who said you go first?" complained Tony.

Christi stepped back flustered. She let Tony take the controls. He made a high score. But when it was her turn, she forgot everything except the screen and the control stick in her hand. All her skill came back. She blew Tony away with her high score. She had a fantastic feeling of being in control. In fact, this new game was almost too easy.

Tony looked at her, impressed. Christi breathed a sigh of relief. Tony punched her on the arm again. "You're really good, Baytony. What other little secrets are you hiding?"

Christi looked up anxiously. She was safe for the moment, but what would Tony and the other guys think if they really knew the secret she was hiding.

"Hey," said Tony. "Lighten up, will ya."

"That's the same advice Phil gave me," admitted Christi.

Tony smiled. "Yeah, well great minds *do* think alike."

Christi grinned at him. She liked Tony. And she couldn't believe that he didn't recognize her. It was as if she had become a different person. Had she? Christi wasn't sure anymore.

Chapter 17
Boys' Dressing Room

Finally, it was Friday, the day of dress rehearsal and Christi was relieved.

"Are you going to make it?" Lizbeth asked. They were in the girls' room cramming for a spelling test the last period. "You look awful."

"I feel awful. I can't believe my lousy luck. How could I get a spelling test on the day of dress rehearsal?"

"It's not fair," said Lizbeth. "Someone told me that Tony DiSpirito got excused from all tests this week because he was working so hard on *Oliver!* It's too bad it's a secret."

"You're telling me," said Christi. "I wish I had known it was going to be this complicated when I started it all."

"Yeah," said Lizbeth. "I feel so sorry for you. You've had to suffer and become friends with Phil Grey and have him tell you that you're talented. It's rough."

Christi punched Lizbeth on the arm.

"Ouch!" cried Lizbeth. "What did you do that for?"

"Sorry," said Christi. "It's just something the guys do all the time to their friends."

"Well, just remember who you're with," said Lizbeth. "Come on. We'd better go, we'll be late."

Christi was relieved that the spelling test was easier than she expected. She knew that she passed it, and she might even have aced it.

As soon as it was over, she rushed over to the Civic Center. The atmosphere backstage had changed dramatically. Everyone was running around at a frantic pace that seemed just this side of hysteria.

"Hey, Chris," shouted Tony. "Come on. They're handing out our costumes."

"Great," said Christi. Then she saw it! A sign on a door that hadn't been there before. BOYS' DRESSING ROOM. Christi cursed herself for not realizing that this was coming. She couldn't go into the *boys'* dressing room. Until now, they had all come dressed in their street clothes. Christi hadn't even thought about how she'd put on her costume, nor had Lizbeth.

Christi could hear laughter coming from the dressing room as the guys tried on their costumes. Wendie was seated behind a long table. She had in front of her piles of urchin suits, divided by sizes. There were only a few left. Nervously, Christi eyed the dwindling pile of costumes. She hung back, but she realized that she was going to have to come forward eventually and claim her costume. She looked once more at the dressing-room door.

Tony slapped her on the back. "This is it," he whispered. "Here's where they separate the men from the boys."

"What does that mean?" exclaimed Christi.

Tony stared at her. "Hey, don't be uptight. I don't know exactly what it means. I just meant we're going into final countdown. Come on, partner, you and I are the best. We don't have a thing to worry about."

Tony winked at her.

Christi wished he were right. She had a lot to worry about. She liked Tony, he'd been a good friend to Chris. Would he be a friend to Christi?

"Come on, kids," said Wendie. "Shake a leg. Phil wants to see you in your costumes as soon as possible." She handed Tony his costume with one hand while she took a sip of a cup of coffee with the other.

A particularly loud burst of laughter came

through the dressing-room door. Christi recognized Jason's laugh. "Hold it down in there!" yelled Wendie.

Christi had visions of naked boys throwing bits and pieces of her costume around the room. She'd have to think of something.

Tony turned to Christi. "Hurry, Baytony. This sounds too good to miss!" Tony grabbed his costume and opened the door to the dressing room just as a new wave of screams and laughs poured out.

Wendie turned towards the dressing room. "Quiet down or I'm coming in there myself!"

Christi saw her chance. Quickly, she knocked over the coffee mug, sending its contents sloshing over the one remaining costume.

"Oh, no," cried Christi, faking horror. "Gosh, I'm so sorry."

Wendie put her hands on her hips and sighed. She gave Christi a dirty look. "Boys, boys, boys! Why couldn't Phil have done *Annie*? We'd have a chorus of cute little orphan girls. Nooo. Phil had to do a revival of *Oliver!*"

Quickly, Christi scooped up the dripping costume. "Don't worry about a thing, Wendie. I'll have this cleaned and back here in a jiffy. My mom's great with stains. I'll take this home to her right now. I'll get it cleaned, and I'll show up back here in costume. Just tell Phil I'll only be a few minutes late."

Before Wendie could answer, Christi darted away just as another burst of laughter came out of the dressing-room door. Christi ran out to the parking lot. She didn't know what to do. Her parents were both at the flower shop. Besides, far from being a magician at getting out spots and stains, her mother hated doing laundry.

Christi threw the costume into her bike basket and headed straight for Lizbeth's house. She didn't even know if Lizbeth was home. All she knew was that she needed help desperately. And Lizbeth was her only chance.

She rang the doorbell insistently. Finally Max came to the door. "Where's the fire?" he asked.

"Max, is Lizbeth home? It's a matter of life or death."

"I thought your finger was stuck on the bell," said Max.

"Who's there?" said Lizbeth from upstairs.

Christi took the stairs two at a time. "It's an emergency," she said. "You gotta help me clean my costume."

Lizbeth gave a warning glance toward Max. "No, my real costume," said Christi urgently. "Can you throw it in the washer and dryer for me and bring it over to the playground near the Civic Center?"

Lizbeth looked at her as if she had gone crazy. "You want me to do laundry for you now?"

"Lizbeth . . . this is a matter of life or death."
Christi looked down. Max was eavesdropping with
an amused expression on his face.

Christi put her lips to Lizbeth's ear. "They've
made one of the rooms a *boys' dressing room*. We
were supposed to all go in there and get dressed.
I couldn't very well change in the *boys'* dressing
room, could I? Could you imagine the scene?"

Lizbeth laughed. "I can imagine it," she said.

"So I spilled coffee all over the costume,"
continued Christi. "I was desperate. But it's got
to be washed and I have to wear it later today.
Just throw it in, and I'll meet you in an hour by
the playground. Okay? And, oh, Lizbeth, don't
worry about ironing it," shouted Christi as she
started down the steps. "Urchins are supposed
to look messy."

Max stopped her as she was running out.
"What's the rush?" he asked.

"I gotta go," said Christi.

Max looked hurt.

"What did you want?" Christi asked.

"Forget it," said Max.

Christi stopped. "No, what is it?"

"Well, I've written my own songs, and I know
you've got a good voice. I wanted to know if you'd
like to sing one I've just written. It's a blues
song. Your voice would be great for it."

Christi felt flattered. Max was paying her a

great compliment. "I can't now," she said. She wished she could tell Max the truth. She'd like to tell him that she was performing in the chorus for Phil Grey, but instead she had to pile one more lie on top of all her others.

"Some other time," said Max. He turned his back on her and went back to the piano.

"Yeah," said Christi. "Some other time."

Max looked at her. "Hey, I have a sweatshirt just like that, and you don't go to Killoleet. Where did you get it?"

Christi looked down at the gray Camp Killoleet sweatshirt. "Oh, my cousin went there. I get all his hand-me-downs."

"Who is he?" asked Max. "I bet I know him."

"No . . . he went there about ten years ago. They're *old* hand-me-downs."

Max looked suspicious. "But they give us a new design each year, and that's the design from two years ago."

Give me a break, Christi thought to herself. "Uh, I guess they must recycle old designs, huh."

"Yeah, I guess so," said Max, sounding doubtful.

"Anyhow," said Christi. "I got to go, but I'd really like to sing your song sometime."

"Okay, sure," said Max, but he still sounded suspicious.

Chapter 18
Feeling Ratty

W hen Christi got back to the auditorium, it took her quite a while to find Tony and the other urchins. The backstage area looked totally chaotic as everyone scrambled around for their props and stopped to stare at each other's costumes.

Tony looked like a nineteenth century imp. He wore dark cotton shorts that were cut with a ragged edge. The costume designer had managed to get twentieth century kids to look like they stepped out of another time. Yet no one piece of clothing was that different from anything worn today. The jackets were nipped at the waist, and the sleeves were a little longer.

The shirts were loose and flowing, a little bit

more like a girl's blouse than a boy's shirt. The urchins weren't dressed in browns and grays, but lavenders, purples, and rosy reds.

"It's like a flower patch of urchins," said Phil, surveying them. He turned to the costume designer. "I love it! It's brilliant." Then his eyes fell on Christi still dressed in jeans and a sweatshirt. "Why aren't you in costume?" he demanded.

"An accident," said Wendie, smiling at Christi. "We spilled coffee on it."

Christi looked at her gratefully. The accident had been her fault. Everyone was being so nice, it made keeping up the lie that much harder.

"I'll have it back in an hour," said Christi.

"Good," said Phil. "I want to see you in it for the final run-through. And *no* baseball cap. I need to see how you all look together. Okay, kids. You can go sit in the audience and watch the run-through until we get to your part. Be quiet out there, and keep your costumes clean."

Tony turned to Christi. "Come on," he said. "This is our only chance to see it from out front."

Christi glanced at her watch. "I got to meet my mother," said Christi. "She's delivering my costume. I told her I'd meet her outside."

"Want me to wait with you?" asked Tony.

"Nah," said Christi, surprised that he would offer.

Tony glanced at her. "Is anything wrong?" he

asked. "You seem real down. You aren't scared about our routine, are you? We got it made."

Christi swallowed hard. "I'm not down," she said defensively.

"Well then you're a good actor," said Tony, punching her on the arm. "You're sure acting the part of a nervous nellie."

Christi laughed, but she didn't think it was funny. She was acting, all the time. She watched Tony go out front to watch the dress rehearsal. She wanted to go with him and sit next to him. There was something special about Tony, something special about her feelings for him. But she could never let Tony know. Christi sighed.

She walked over to the playground. She hoped Lizbeth wouldn't be late. She looked around anxiously. There were a few small children playing on the teeter-totters and merry-go-rounds.

Christi stood at the bottom of a large slide. Suddenly a bookbag stuffed with her costume came zooming down the slide. It slammed into the back of Christi's knees, sending her sprawling into the sandpit at the bottom of the slide.

Christi turned and looked back over her shoulder. Lizbeth was perched at the top of the giant slide.

"Lizbeth! Cut out the spy stuff, okay?"

"Okay! Okay! I was just trying not to blow your cover," shouted Lizbeth. "Sorry, Christi."

Lizbeth came down the slide, feet first. "Don't bother to thank me for practically risking my life by stealing my own brother's clothes so you can be a star. Don't bother to thank me for doing your laundry. It hasn't been easy, you know . . . this handmaiden-to-the-star routine."

Christi looked chastened. "Well, you won't have to do it very much longer anyway. In fact, it will all be over sooner than you think."

"Oh, no!" cried Lizbeth. "Did one of the boys find out? What happened?"

"Nothing like that. But . . . well, fooling everybody just doesn't seem like such a good idea anymore."

"I absolutely do not believe you are saying this." Lizbeth picked up the bookbag full of clothes. They started to walk back towards the Civic Center.

"I don't either," said Christi. "But it just isn't working out like I thought it would. Phil Grey's been so nice to me, and all I've done is lie to him. And lie to my parents. They want to come backstage after the performance and meet Phil Grey. How am I going to stop my father from saying something dumb like, 'I'm so proud of my little girl'?"

"Maybe you can tell your parents that Phil Grey isn't letting anyone backstage." Lizbeth paused. "Except me, of course. If, after all I've done, I don't get to meet Phil Grey, I'll die. To think, for two whole weeks you've had to be around all those creepy guys, especially Tony DiSpirito, and now you're not even happy."

"The guys aren't so creepy. They're really okay. They're not jerks like we thought. Tony, especially, is really nice."

"Oh, great," said Lizbeth angrily. "Now you and Tony DiSpirito are best friends."

"It's not that," said Christi, warily, realizing that Lizbeth was jealous.

"Then what is it?"

"I don't know, I feel like we're being ratty by tricking everybody—Phil Grey, my parents, Tony, and the other guys in the chorus."

Lizbeth stopped dead in her tracks. "Swell! So now I'm 'really ratty' and Tony DiSpirito is 'really okay'! Maybe you'd like him as a boyfriend. Well, he's only being nice to you because he thinks you're Chris Bayton, a boy. Why don't you tell him you're Christi Bay and see how nice he is then?"

Furiously, Lizbeth shoved the bookbag at Christi and stomped off. Christi watched her best friend go. She realized she had never felt so alone in her life. Her best friend in the world thought she was awful for liking boys, and her new friends, the boys, would hate her if they knew the truth, that she was a girl.

Chapter 19
No Amateurs Allowed

Christi slipped into the ladies' room and emptied out the bookbag to put on her costume. She saw the lavender pants and jacket, but the rose-red shirt wasn't there. Christi shook out the bottom of the bag to make sure.

She felt desperate. She picked up the phone and called Lizbeth, hoping that Lizbeth wasn't so mad that she wouldn't help her anymore.

"Max, it's me, Christi. It's an emergency. Is Lizbeth there?"

"She went to meet you," said Max. "What's the emergency now? What's going on between you two?"

Christi felt like crying. Could she dare tell Max

what she was doing? She had to get that missing part of her costume.

"Christi, can I help you?" Max sounded sincere. Christi hesitated. Could she trust him, a boy?

Christi sighed. It was just too complicated to explain. "No, thanks, Max, but I need Lizbeth."

"Well, you're in luck. I see Her Highness coming up the driveway now."

"Thank goodness! Max, can you tell her to hurry?"

Christi waited impatiently for Lizbeth to get on the phone. It seemed to take hours.

"Christi? Now what?" asked Lizbeth.

"Part of my costume is missing. You forgot the shirt, the rose-colored shirt for my costume. Someone will notice! I know you're mad at me, but I need the shirt. Phil Grey wants to see us in our costumes."

Lizbeth paused. "I'm getting a little tired of being needed," she said frostily.

"Lizbeth, please," pleaded Christi. "I can't go out there like this. I'm desperate."

"You've been a little too desperate."

"I know," sighed Christi. Finally, she thought of a plan that would appeal to Lizbeth. "Look, don't you want to come to the theater? I'll try to slip you in so you can see Phil Grey."

"Where are we going to meet? You don't want to be seen with a *girl*, do you?"

Christi thought furiously. She glanced around. She saw a door labeled PROP ROOM. It was the place where props were stored from earlier productions. Nobody would be going in there. It would be the perfect place to meet Lizbeth.

"Come to the theater," whispered Christi. "Go directly backstage. I've gotten to know Wendie. I'll tell her you're bringing something for me. We can meet in the old prop room. Nobody ever goes there. It'll be safe."

"Safe from what? I thought those boys were such good friends of yours."

"Lizbeth, it's not like that, honest. Please help me. I'll find a way to introduce you to Phil, okay?"

Lizbeth hesitated. "Well . . ."

"I'll tell him you're my best friend," urged Christi, sensing that Lizbeth was weakening.

"Well, all right," said Lizbeth. "But give me a minute. I have to figure out what to wear."

"Don't take too long. We're due on stage for our routine in just a few minutes."

Christi hurried out into the corridor. She saw Tony and a group of boys coming towards her. She couldn't risk talking to them now. Quickly Christi slipped into the prop room, praying that Tony hadn't seen her.

The prop room was dimly lit, and full of dust. The room was jammed full of furniture from old productions, sofas, and medieval thrones. There was even an old apple tree made out of cardboard. There were also about a dozen mannequins that the designers used to design costumes for other productions. Christi slumped down in a tattered wing chair to wait for Lizbeth. She bit her fingernails. She couldn't believe that everything was such a mess.

Suddenly, the door opened. Christi jumped up and moved towards the door. Then she froze. She heard Tony's voice.

"This place is neat . . . all dark and spooky. It's full of all kinds of junk," said Tony.

"Let's check it out," said Bobby. "They're testing lighting. It's boring out there. Let's see what's in here. I've been meaning to check this room out all week."

"I don't know," said Jason. "We're supposed to be where Phil can find us."

The door stayed partially open. Christi held her breath and prayed that they would decide not to come in.

"We got time," said Tony. "I agree with Bobby. It's boring out front. Besides, I've set my watch for the time that Phil wants us out front. We don't have to worry. Let's explore this place. Bet there's some really weird stuff in here."

Christi glanced around hoping for a possible escape or a place to hide. There wasn't any. A mannequin caught her eye and suddenly she assumed the same stiff, spread-fingered pose. She held her breath.

Tony and three of the other urchins piled into the prop room. They discovered a pile of rubber swords. "Hey, look at this!" shouted Bobby.

He picked up one of the swords. "On guard!" he shouted. He flung a sword to Tony. Tony caught it deftly, and they began to act out a mock duel.

Suddenly the room was filled with a high-pitched beeping. It was Tony's watch.

"Rehearsal's going to start."

Bobby continued to prance around, parrying and lunging, coming dangerously close to Christi, but his back was turned to her. "Who cares?" said Bobby. "They're running so late. They won't need us for hours yet."

"Come on, Bobby," said Tony angrily. "Suppose you're wrong? You know what Phil said about us being on time!"

Bobby fumbled and dropped his sword. He bent down to pick it up, stepping right on Christi's foot as he did. She stifled a scream. It hurt!

Without looking up, Bobby reached down, scooped up his sword and tossed it back on the pile. He followed the others to the door. Tony opened the door, and just then Lizbeth stumbled into the room.

At first she was too shocked to speak.

"What are you doin' here, Lizbeth?" asked Tony.

Lizbeth couldn't think of anything to say.

Tony looked at her curiously. "Whatever it is, you better beat it. This show is still boys only."

Lizbeth frantically grasped for a snappy comeback.

"Oh yeah, well you can keep it. Nobody is going to want to see a play with dumb boys in it."

"Oh yeah," said Tony. "Well, we'll keep it, 'cause we already *got* it."

"What you got, nobody wants," snapped Lizbeth.

Tony laughed at her. "Well, what we got, Phil Grey wants, and he doesn't want to see you. Backstage is strictly for us professionals. No amateurs allowed."

"They don't make them any more amateur than you, Tony DiSpirito."

"Yeah," sneered Tony. "Well, I've got a part in this play, and you and your little sissy friend Christi with your big crushes on Phil Grey, you can't get near him. 'Cause you're a girl. Now, excuse us, we've got a show to put on."

Tony pushed past Lizbeth triumphantly, leaving her staring at a very strange-looking mannequin in the back of the prop room.

Chapter 20
Partners Gotta Stick Together

"Christi, are you all right?" asked Lizbeth, as Christi slowly twisted her neck around trying to relieve the tension.

"Barely," answered Christi. She shook out her fingers. They were stiff and cramped from holding them still for so long. "I can't stand any more of these close calls."

"Well, it'll be over soon," said Lizbeth. She sank down into the wing chair. "Thank goodness, I'm not sure I like you half-boy half-girl."

Christi shook her head. "I'm sorry. I've treated you pretty rotten."

Lizbeth smiled. "Well, I guess every star has someone like me to run around for them. All it's

113

taught me is that I'd rather be a star."

Christi laughed.

"See, now you seem like your old self again. I just don't like you as a boy."

"That's not the problem," Christi said. "To tell the truth, boys have fun. They're not so bad. The problem is me. All the lying has made me act creepy to everyone. You, Phil, the guys here . . . my folks. I made a good boy. I was just a lousy person."

"I wouldn't take it that far," said Lizbeth.

Christi looked at her watch. "I've got to put on that shirt. I'm supposed to be on stage."

Lizbeth took out Christi's shirt. She had even ironed it. Christi was touched. "Thanks," she said, quickly slipping it on.

She looked at Lizbeth. "I think I'm going to tell them the truth."

"Christi! After all we've been through. It's *one* more night."

"I know. But I can't make it one more night. Maybe the boys-only rule wasn't fair, but what I'm doing isn't fair, either. I hate tricking people who believe in me. It doesn't feel good. Today is my last day, Lizbeth."

"You sound like you're going to the guillotine."

Christi giggled. "I guess I was taking myself a little too seriously. But I *am* going to tell."

"If you do, they might kick you out of the show."

"I know, and that'll leave the chorus short one person. How did things get so complicated?"

"God should never have created men *and* women," said Lizbeth.

"I wouldn't go that far," said Christi. "Come on, I think this is going to be your last chance to meet Phil Grey."

"The play's tomorrow. I mean, are you sure you can't go just one more day?"

Christi blinked. "Yeah, I'm sure," she said quietly. "Phil hates it when you're late. It's not professional. I've got to go."

"I don't think he's gonna think what you've been doing is too professional," warned Lizbeth.

Phil was perched on a stool at center stage. He called for the urchins to gather around him for their final meeting. Lizbeth hung back in the shadows of the wings.

Tony waved to Christi. He moved over, saving her a space next to him. Phil smiled at her.

"Well, guys, we made it," he said. "We survived, and we're going to have an excellent production of *Oliver!* And a lot of the credit for that goes to you. It's been super working with you guys . . . all of you. Everyone of you has a special kind of talent. I'm proud to have been able to help you develop a little. You're good actors and good people. It's been great to be with you. You're open, honest."

Christi cringed at the word "honest."

Phil grinned at them. It was the same smile she had seen on screen so many times, but now he just looked like an ordinary person with a nice smile.

Tony began to applaud. The rest of the urchins joined in, clapping and cheering. Christi clapped until her hands were red, but she felt like crying, too.

Phil actually began to blush. "Thanks for letting me hang around with you guys. You taught me a lot about what kids are like today . . . and believe me, it's not all bad. Now, let's go. We've got a show to do!"

He stood up. Wendie dashed over and handed him a clipboard and a pen. "Phil, can you sign off on the lighting cues for the finale?"

"Yeah, as long as they bring the whole look down about a half step."

Christi took a step forward. "Phil, I need . . ."

Phil waved her away. "Later, Chris. Oh, Wendie, tell Jack to be sure that breakaway chair is . . ."

"But, Phil, I've gotta . . ."

Phil looked annoyed. "Chris, we're about to start dress rehearsal. This isn't the time for a heart-to-heart talk. Remember what I said about you guys being pros?"

Christi fought back tears. "I am a pro, but I've got to talk to you."

Wendie broke in. She too looked very annoyed at Christi. "Phil, they need you backstage."

"It'll just take a minute!" cried Christi.

Phil had already turned to go backstage. He scowled. "Chris, you're acting like a spoiled baby. Try to act like what you are—an eleven-year-old boy."

Christi felt as if she was going to explode. "But that's what I've been trying to tell you . . . *I'm not!*" she screamed.

Phil stopped in his tracks. The urchins, Wendie, and everyone else on stage fell silent. No one, including Christi, seemed to know what to say next. Tony stepped over to Christi, moving closer, as if to protect his buddy. But he looked embarrassed and confused.

Finally, Tony spoke. "Hey, what's the big deal, Baytony? Got opening night nerves?" Tony tried to laugh, but it came out more as a cough. He was trying to help. He was being a good friend, but Christi knew he didn't understand.

"It's not nerves . . ." Christi swallowed hard. Tony *was* the only one who could help her now. She took off her glasses and cap. "Remember how you kept saying you thought you knew me? You do. I sit in front of you in glee club."

Tony opened his mouth. For several seconds he couldn't speak. Then his eyes focused on Lizbeth standing in the corner. *"Christi Bay! and Lizbeth!* What a sneaky thing to do!"

Phil Grey noticed Lizbeth for the first time. "Who's she? What's she doing here?" He asked accusingly. "What's going on?"

Lizbeth looked as if she wanted to sink through the stage. Christi went and stood beside her. "She's my best friend. She helped me. Tony's right. I was sneaky. I knew I was good enough to be in the play. I just wanted to be able to try out, and then when they said 'boys only,' I couldn't think of any other way. So Lizbeth and I cooked up this scheme. But we didn't think it would hurt anybody."

Christi paused. "Besides, I used to think boys were just dumb jerks and tricking them wouldn't matter, but you're not. You're my friends, and I couldn't keep on lying to you, so . . ."

Christi turned, and spoke looking into Phil's eyes. "So, I'm sorry. Really. I just wanted to be able to work with you. And they said I couldn't . . . just because I was a girl. It made me mad that it didn't even matter if I was good or not." Christi swallowed again hard. She would *not* cry!

"You sure are one little actress," said Phil, staring at her.

Christi hung her head. "I'm sorry. That's all I can say."

"Maybe, that's not all," said Phil.

"What do you mean?"

"I've got to say you had me fooled and that takes some kind of acting. You are good, Chris. And you might be right. Maybe I stuck to the script too arbitrarily. There are no good reasons why there couldn't have been girl urchins as well as boys in Dickens' day. I bet plenty of young girls were homeless, too. We can all make mistakes. I'd like you to stay."

Christi brightened. "Really!"

"But it's not entirely up to me. The guys in the chorus are the ones who'll have to work with you. They're the ones who'll have to decide."

No one said anything for a moment. Christi looked around at the guys. They avoided her glance. She looked at Tony, but he too was silent, and he looked angry.

"I don't know," said Bobby finally. "It was pretty sneaky. I should have guessed. I don't want to work with a girl, not one who'd pull a stunt like that."

"You should have guessed, but you didn't," said Tony. "Neither did I. None of us did." He turned to Chris. "I don't know how you did it."

Christi shrugged her shoulders. "I didn't do anything *that* unusual."

Tony fixed Christi with a steely gaze. "You blew out my high score at the arcade. You never did learn how to pop a decent wheelie. . . ."

Tony paused, looking around at his captive audience, obviously loving the dramatic effect that his words were having.

"But . . ." he said, moving a step closer to Christi so that they were almost nose to nose. "But, you're still my partner, and partners gotta stick together. Okay, Christi Bay. You're in."

Christi jumped up and down. "Oh, thank you," she squealed. She was about to hug him, and then she stopped herself just as her arms were in midair on either side of him. She whipped her arms down and wiped the smile from her face.

She lowered her voice. "Thanks, DiSpirito." Then she slugged him on the arm, really slugged him. Tony went sprawling at Phil Grey's feet.

Phil laughed. "Somehow I think this is where I came in," he said.

Chapter 21

Everything's Coming Up Roses

The next morning, Christi woke up with the delicious sweet smell of roses in her room. The dress rehearsal had gone on until midnight, and she hadn't had a chance to talk to her parents afterwards.

She rubbed her eyes and looked at her clock radio. It said 1 PM. She had thought that she would be too excited to sleep, but she hadn't. She had actually slept for almost ten hours. She couldn't believe it.

She looked across the room. A huge vase full of roses sat on her dresser. Christi got up and looked at it. There was a florist card stuck in the flowers. Christi opened the card. "Everything is going to come up roses tonight! Sleep all day if you want to. All our love, Mom and Dad."

Christi put the card back into the roses. She smelled them. They were just beautiful. And then she sighed. She was due at the theater at four o'clock. But she knew there was something she had to do before then.

She got dressed and went downstairs. The house seemed so quiet. They were weaving carnations into the wire mold when her mom saw her in the doorway.

Her father quickly stepped in front of the display when he saw her. "Christi . . . we didn't expect you down here today. Today's your day! Go back upstairs and relax."

Christi picked up a carnation and started to stick it into the mold. She loved helping her parents do those giant creations, and she knew that they rarely got orders for them.

"Who's this for?"

"*Rotary*!" said her father loudly and quickly. Her mother nodded her head vigorously.

Christi looked at them curiously.

"Honey," said her mother, moving Christi away from the horseshoe. "I really do think you should go back upstairs. We'll take a break and come up and see you in just a little while."

"Uhh . . . but there's something I've got to talk to you about," said Christi.

Christi's parents looked at each other. "Let's close up the shop," said her dad. "Today's a special day. 'We're closed for a while due to a star in the family.' Come on, let's go upstairs."

Quickly her father hustled Christi out. He flipped the OPEN sign on the door to CLOSED, and locked up.

They went upstairs. Her mother poured Christi a big glass of fresh orange juice. "This will give you strength for tonight. Remember to drink the vitamins."

Christi smiled. When she was little her mother had told her that all the vitamins fell to the bottom of the glass, and she had believed her until last year in biology when she learned that vitamins were suspended in liquids. It had become a family joke.

"Do you have opening night nerves?" asked her father. "Don't worry, I bet even Phil Grey is nervous right now."

Christi stared at her glass. "No, it's not nerves. I've got to tell you something."

Her mother laughed nervously. "What is it? You're going to run away to New York and be the star."

"No, Mom . . . it's not a joke. Well, it sort of started as a joke. But I've got to tell you how I got this part."

"You got it on talent," said her father.

"Well, partially," said Christi. "But I also got it 'cause I pretended to be a boy."

Her parents stared at her. "Christi, what are you talking about?"

Christi explained about the boys-only audition. She told them about Lizbeth helping her with the disguises.

"You deceived everybody," exclaimed her mother.

Christi nodded. "I didn't like it."

"I should hope not," said her father. "I don't like it either. I imagine Phil Grey was very angry. I'm pretty angry. I don't like the fact that you lied to us, either."

"I thought I had to lie," said Christi. "It wasn't fair that they wouldn't let girls try out. Phil was kind of mad at first. But he realized that I had to be a very good actress to pull it off. He let the boys in the chorus decide if I could stay. And they said 'yes.' So now, I guess it's up to you. You can forbid me."

Christi looked scared.

Her mother and father looked at each other. "You want to be in this performance very badly, don't you?"

Christi nodded. "More than anything I've ever wanted in my whole life."

Her father looked Christi in the eye. "Well, I don't think it's our job to go against Phil Grey's decision. If he still wants you, I think you've learned your lesson about lying. However, I have to tell you, I don't like it." He looked at Christi. "And I never liked your hair."

"Neither did I," admitted Christi. "I just wanted the part so badly."

"Well," said her mother. "You certainly showed ambition. You never gave up."

"It wasn't easy," admitted Christi. "Wait till you hear the whole story."

When she got to the part about getting the guys to respect her by beating them at the video arcade, her mother began to smile.

"I always knew that talent would come in handy someday."

The more Christi talked, the funnier the whole episode seemed. She got to the part about how Lizbeth insisted on wearing her own disguises to hand her Max's clothes, and she couldn't help laughing.

Her parents started to laugh, too.

Then she told her parents how she had begun to feel bad about deceiving everybody and that she had finally told Phil Grey and the others the truth.

"They decided they still wanted me to be in the play," said Christi. "But I thought I should tell you the truth, too."

Her father tried to look serious. Then he burst

125

out laughing. "I'm sorry," he said. "It was just the idea of you and Lizbeth in your disguises. I agree with Phil Grey. I think it proves you're a very good actress. And do you want to know something, I'm proud of you."

"Proud that I tricked everybody?"

Her father shook his head. "No, proud that you're the kind of girl . . . person, who didn't feel good tricking everyone. I'm proud that you decided to tell the truth. But I'm also proud that you're the kind of a kid who doesn't like dumb rules."

Her mother nodded. "Me, too. I'm not happy that you didn't come to us sooner and tell us about it. But, all in all, I think you did the right thing, both in trying out and in coming clean." Then she burst out laughing. "I just wish I could have seen you in full disguise."

"You can," said Christi. "I've still got it. Wait a minute."

Christi ran upstairs and for the last time put on Max's smelly, too large Nikes and his old rugby shirt, and then she put on her glasses and her baseball cap.

She looked at herself in the mirror, and she saw the huge bouquet of roses. She plucked out one of the roses, and put it in the buttonhole of her rugby shirt. Then she went into the kitchen

and ran through all her routines for her parents.
For her finale, Christi kicked off the Nikes, and
then did a deep bow.

Her parents applauded and then they all burst
out laughing.

Chapter 22
Go as Yourself

"I think I'm going to throw up," said Tony when Christi arrived at the theater for opening night.

"Be cool," said Christi. "Remember, partner, we're the best."

Tony frowned. "How can you say that?"

"Because we've got the best of both worlds. We're the only co-ed urchins in the chorus."

Tony laughed. "I still think I might throw up," he said.

"Don't worry," said Christi. "All good performers have stage fright. It'll just make us better."

"Are you nervous, too?" asked Tony.

"Scared to death," admitted Christi.

"I wish you'd act it."

"I'm a good actress, remember? Believe me, the sides of my stomach are playing racketball with each other."

Tony held his hand out. Christi slapped it.

Finally, they heard the orchestra start the overture. Christi shook her hands at her sides, trying to loosen up. Then she heard their cue. Tony glanced at her. "Good luck," he whispered.

"You, too," Christi whispered back. Then she did something that shocked him. She kissed him on the cheek. Tony blushed. Then he kissed her back. "Let's go," he whispered.

They rushed on stage. Christi could hardly remember the performance. It seemed to go by in a flash.

Finally, she and the chorus joined Phil and the stars for the finale of "I'd Do Anything for You!" The entire audience burst into applause. Christi couldn't see anything beyond the footlights, but she heard someone shouting, "EXCELLENT! EXCELLENT!" and she recognized Lizbeth's voice.

The entire cast went out for a final curtain call, and Christi's costume was drenched with sweat.

Then the curtain fell. Phil Grey gathered everybody around. He winked at Christi. "You guys were almost perfect," he said. "I mean it. I just have a few notes for you. A few changes I want to make for tomorrow night's performance."

But before he could begin to speak, Wendie wheeled in a huge floral display in the shape of a giant star.

Phil stared at it. "What's this?"

"It was delivered just now. The florists are here. I gave them permission to give it to you in person."

"I don't want to see anybody now," snapped Phil.

"I think these flowers are special," insisted Wendie. Christi looked in the wings and saw her parents and the Collins family waving nervously.

Phil walked over to the horseshoe. He read the ribbon and burst out laughing.

"GOOD LUCK TO PHIL GREY AND THE URCHINS— BOYS AND GIRL!"

He looked at Christi. "Did you have something to do with this?"

"My parents," said Christi, embarrassed. "They're the florists." She brought her parents over and introduced them to Phil Grey. "Mom and Dad, I want you to meet Phil Grey."

Phil shook their hands. "I think the flowers are beautiful. I've seen old movies where the stars got flower arrangements like that, but I've never gotten one in my life and I've always wanted one."

"We've always wanted to make one," said her

mother. "We just never knew a star to give it to."

"I think you might have one in the family," said Phil. "You've got a talented girl," he said. "Sort of like a preteen Tootsie in reverse."

Mr. Bay laughed.

Christi took Lizbeth's hand and brought her forward. "You've met Lizbeth. This is her mother, and her brother Max." Christi looked at Max guiltily. "Max contributed to my disguise, only he didn't know about it. I borrowed your clothes, your hat, and your shoes."

"My Killoleet sweatshirt!" cried Max.

"Max is a great musician," said Christi quickly. "Someday, Phil, you should hear his songs."

Max gave Phil an embarrassed smile.

"I'd like to hear you sometime," said Phil. "I'm always interested in new talent."

"And Lizbeth is my very best friend. I couldn't have done it without her. She cut my hair and planned my wardrobe. I owe it all to her."

Phil Grey leaned down and shook her hand. "You may have a career in costume design," he said smiling. "You sure fooled me."

Lizbeth blushed. Then she brought out her autograph book. "Can I have your autograph?" she asked.

Tony groaned. He and the other guys had made

such an effort to be cool and not ask Phil Grey for his autograph. The other guys all groaned, too. Christi felt herself turn red.

"Shut up, guys," said Phil, taking Lizbeth's book. "I'd love to. You know nobody's asked me to sign an autograph all week. I've kind of missed it."

With that, all the guys in the chorus rushed to get their programs. Phil signed the programs of each and every guy in the chorus. Christi and Tony were the last in line.

Phil took Tony's program. "DiSpirito, you've got a lot of talent, too. And you and Christi make a good team." Phil winked. "You know, girls aren't so bad. Take it from me."

Christi looked at Tony. He was blushing.

Then Phil took Christi's program. He ran his finger down the page and then he burst into a big grin. In the cast list for the urchin chorus, Chris Bayton had been crossed out and the name Christine Bay written in beside it.

Phil Grey picked up his pen. "To Christi, you're going to go far. Next time, just remember to go as yourself. Love, Phil."

He handed it back to Christi. She took it from him and read what he had written. Then she gave Phil a hug. Tony was standing beside her. Before he could move, she turned and hugged him, too.

About the Author

ELIZABETH LEVY grew up in Buffalo but has been a resident of New York City for 20 years. She began her career as a TV news researcher and has been a teacher and an editor. Now she devotes her time to writing. She is the author of the popular GYMNASTS series as well as *The Computer That Said Steal Me* and other books published by Scholastic.

APPLE® PAPERBACKS

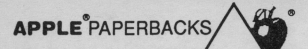

Pick an Apple and Polish Off Some Great Reading!

BEST-SELLING APPLE TITLES

❏ MT43944-8 **Afternoon of the Elves** Janet Taylor Lisle $2.

❏ MT43109-9 **Boys Are Yucko** Anna Grossnickle Hines $2.

❏ MT43473-X **The Broccoli Tapes** Jan Slepian $2.

❏ MT40961-1 **Chocolate Covered Ants** Stephen Manes $2.

❏ MT45436-6 **Cousins** Virginia Hamilton $2.

❏ MT44036-5 **George Washington's Socks** Elvira Woodruff $2

❏ MT45244-4 **Ghost Cadet** Elaine Marie Alphin $2.

❏ MT44351-8 **Help! I'm a Prisoner in the Library** Eth Clifford $2

❏ MT43618-X **Me and Katie (The Pest)** Ann M. Martin $2

❏ MT43030-0 **Shoebag** Mary James $2

❏ MT46075-7 **Sixth Grade Secrets** Louis Sachar $2

❏ MT42882-9 **Sixth Grade Sleepover** Eve Bunting $2

❏ MT41732-0 **Too Many Murphys** Colleen O'Shaughnessy McKenna $2